Treasured by a Tiger

Felicity Heaton

ETERNAL MATES SERIES

Kissed by a Dark Prince
Claimed by a Demon King
Tempted by a Rogue Prince
Hunted by a Jaguar
Craved by an Alpha
Bitten by a Hellcat
Taken by a Dragon
Marked by an Assassin
Possessed by a Dark Warrior
Awakened by a Demoness
Haunted by the King of Death
Turned by a Tiger
Tamed by a Tiger
Treasured by a Tiger
Unchained by a Forbidden Love – Coming in 2017

Find out more at: www.felicityheaton.co.uk

CHAPTER 1

Curiosity killed the cat.

It was always there, in the back of Grey's mind.

Although this time, it was his twin's curiosity that might get him killed.

Black lands stretched as far as the eye could see around him, the sky a dull gold that was growing brighter as he trekked closer to the realm that fiery glow emanated from. Not like he wanted to go anywhere near that damned place, but it seemed the trail he was following wanted to lead him straight towards it.

Grey looked over his shoulder at the distant blue glow that King Thorne of the Third Realm of demons had told him belonged to the elf kingdom. Fucking place sounded magical. Why couldn't Talon's itch have led Grey in that direction?

Lush green hills, towering grey mountains, glittering blue streams, and all the sunshine their portal could pour into their kingdom.

He would have given anything to be there, stretched out on the long grass, soaking up that sun and letting the cool breeze play over his bare skin.

Instead, he was trudging through a wasteland, his feet sore in his black leather boots, and the sweat pouring off him sticking his black t-shirt to his skin.

All for his brother's sake.

He rolled his stiff shoulders, grimacing as a few vertebrae cracked.

Maybe not all for Talon.

The thought of being at the pride village now that his sister, Maya, was gone to be with her fated one, August, had driven him to leave, to find somewhere else to be.

Maybe somewhere he belonged.

He had ended up at Underworld, the nightclub Talon now called home because his fated mate worked there. Grey didn't belong there though. A few quiet days had passed before that restless itch had pushed him to keep moving, and he still wasn't sure where he was meant to be going.

He was lost.

He exhaled hard.

Not a sigh.

He might not be sure where he was meant to be going, but his feet were carrying him forwards anyway, and if he had to keep walking forever until he found that place they wanted to rest, he would.

Talon had given him a new direction at least.

Over dinner one night, Talon had mentioned seeing the door again in his dreams. Sherry had given her mate a concerned look, one Grey hadn't missed. He had focused on his brother then, and felt that need flowing through him, that curiosity that wouldn't let him go, not until he knew what was beyond that door.

It wouldn't have been a problem, but the door in question was deep in the bowels of the headquarters of a mortal hunter organisation, a building where Talon had been held captive and tortured for months.

Grey was damned if he was going to let his brother go back into that hellish place.

So, when Sherry had mentioned looking through the files they had stolen from Archangel when breaking Talon's friends out, Grey had leaped at the chance to help. He would do anything for his brother.

Including going to Hell in his place.

The moment he had found the door mentioned in one of the project files, and uncovered that it was connected to something in Hell, he had known what he needed to do.

Where he had to be.

Talon needed to know what was beyond that door, and Grey was going to find out for him.

His twin had fought him on that, which hadn't been a surprise given Talon's habit of trying to act like his big brother. The bastard was stubborn and pushy, had been like it since birth when he had muscled his way out first, arriving in the world a whole eight minutes ahead of Grey.

Eight minutes did not an older brother make.

Grey could be just as stubborn though, and eventually Talon had given in, Sherry convincing him to let Grey go to Hell in his place and follow up their lead.

He had left immediately.

He would find out what was beyond that door even if it killed him. He would do that for Talon, to put his mind at rest and free him from the clutches of his curiosity.

He sighed and looked back over his shoulder, in the direction of the Third Realm and the elf kingdom beyond it. Although, it still would have been nice if Thorne had told him to head that way instead of towards the Devil's lands.

A cold sinking feeling had gone through him in the demon king's library when the huge russet-haired male had jabbed a strong clawed finger against a mountain range and told him that was where he needed to start, because it was the place mentioned in one of the reports linked to the project.

Grey hadn't failed to notice that east of that mountain range was labelled as the dragon realm, and beyond that was the Devil's domain.

Thorne had been generous enough to offer him an escort.

It had felt like a kick in the balls at the time.

Even Sable, the demon's little queen and ex-Archangel hunter, had flinched at the offer, and had dished him out an apologetic glance.

Grey had refused Thorne, because he had grown tired of being coddled by his brothers a long time ago, and wasn't about to accept it from a male he barely knew.

Looking back, he probably should have taken the demon up on his kind offer. The big guy had been nice enough to teleport him into Hell, had put him up for a few days at his castle, and had sent him off with some provisions and a crudely drawn map of Hell.

Grey pulled the map out of the thigh pocket of his black combat trousers and stared at it.

At how close the village was to dragons and the Devil.

A few demonic travelling companions probably wouldn't have been a bad thing.

It wasn't as if he knew Hell. He had come here without a plan, without any idea about what to expect, and that was dangerous.

His family had raised him to be prepared.

It had all gone out the window when Maya had left, and that feeling had kicked in, that need to walk and not stop walking, to put as much distance as he could between him and his pride.

He pressed his hand flat against his chest, felt his heart thumping hard against his palm, and stared into the distance, not seeing the cragged mountains that speared the gold sky.

What was it that had made him leave?

He was mad at his older brother, the alpha of their pride, and needed some space and time to work through those feelings. Mostly because he wanted to throat-punch Byron whenever he saw him.

Was that the reason he had strayed this far from home?

He didn't want to do something he would regret?

As much as he hated Byron right now, which the bastard deserved after everything that Maya had been through because of him, he still loved the son of a bitch. He was still Grey's brother.

Grey started walking again, his hand drifting across his chest to adjust the straps of his backpack. He jammed his thumb through the right strap and let his hand dangle there, his mind whirling as he thought about home and the gnawing feeling in the depths of his heart. Something had made him leave. Something other than his anger towards Byron.

Had to be.

Gods, maybe he was just messed up.

More fucked up than he had thought possible.

Or maybe there was nothing keeping him at the pride now.

It was strange having his freedom after spending two centuries at the pride, devoted to the care and protection of his little sister. He couldn't remember a time when he had been free to come and go as he pleased. It had been erased from his memories, replaced by the decades that had come after Byron had become alpha, a time when Grey had been locked away from the world because Byron had deemed it too dangerous for Maya to be allowed to go outside the pride village, and had charged him with being at her side always.

Meaning the bastard had shut them both in a cage.

Fuck, it was weird.

Was that why he felt lost?

Because he was free at last?

He still hadn't processed that, wasn't sure he would for a long time yet. He had never really felt like a captive, because his family had been there, everyone he cared about at the village with him, but now that he was free to come and go as he pleased, he felt as if he had been a captive his entire life.

The world beyond the one he had known was huge, endless, filled with incredible things and possibilities, and he had hurled himself headlong into that world.

It was a little overwhelming.

His senses sparked, warning of life nearby, and he tensed and stilled, stretching his focus outwards to encompass the area. He slowed his breathing, becoming silent in the shadowy world, and his vision brightened as he studied the dimly-lit lands surrounding him, making it easier for him to pick out the rocks that could easily hide enemies, giving them ample chance to sneak up on him.

He should have taken Thorne up on his offer.

But the thought of having a demon escort had felt like another cage.

He wanted to be free.

He curled his lip and dragged air over his teeth, trying to scent the owner of that heartbeat.

Another joined it as he risked a step closer, and then a third and a fourth.

He peered ahead of him, into the darkness.

Something was there.

He risked another two steps.

The shadowy shapes came into focus.

Huts.

The village Thorne had said was the one Archangel had named in their report.

He must have walked further than he had realised while lost in his thoughts.

Grey cautiously moved forwards, lowering his hands to his sides as he approached the village. The loose black gravel crunched under his heavy boots, loud in the thick still air, grating at him. His muscles twitched beneath his skin and an urge to shift settled over him as he closed in on the buildings and the people coming and going between them.

It had been more than a day since he had last seen people, a day of trekking across a black wasteland with only an occasional distant screech or roar punctuating the silence. Those sounds had raked at his nerves, leaving them raw and stealing sleep from him. He hadn't rested in more than twenty-four hours.

It was little wonder he felt on edge now.

Ready for a fight.

He felt vulnerable, easy prey if anyone chose to fight him, his body and mind badly in need of rest.

For all he knew, those sounds that had kept him marching forwards rather than taking a break could have been made by people. Hell was full of things he had never seen before, creatures straight out of myths and legends, or horror movies.

He could be walking right into a nest of the howling, shrieking beasts, lured into a false sense of security by their human appearances.

The urge to shift into his stronger form to protect himself grew stronger, and he slowly pulled down another calming breath. He was letting his imagination run away with him, and that was dangerous.

He needed answers, and kicking up a fuss in his tiger form just because he feared the things that had gone bump in the night in the wasteland wasn't going to get him any, especially if the people in the village found out he thought they were the ones making those unholy noises.

He doubted they were.

It was just his imagination tricking his weary mind into believing something ridiculous—something liable to get him killed.

He needed to rest and regain some strength, and then his imagination wouldn't hold such sway over him.

He didn't need to shift.

He kept it tamped down, breathing through it and tightening his hold on his control, refusing to let his tiger instincts rule him. He was only here to speak with the people and find out what they knew about the project, and what Archangel had wanted when they had come through this way.

He wasn't here to fight.

The urge to shift didn't abate as he entered the village perimeter, marked by a rough stone wall that circled the few black huts and makeshift tents made of some sort of animal hide. If anything, it grew stronger in time with the scents of the people coming and going through the settlement.

Some of them were powerful.

Some smelled of the tinny scent of magic.

A dark-haired male dressed in long black robes off to his right stopped hammering a peg for his tent into the inky dirt and looked up at Grey.

A witch. Or did they prefer warlock? Wizard?

What the hell did they like being called? He could hardly go and speak to the male if he wasn't sure. The last thing he needed to do was insult someone who could flay him with nothing more than a few muttered words.

Grey shuddered as he looked at the male's hands.

And realised the tent peg he had been hammering into the black ground wasn't the sort bought in a store in the mortal world.

It was a broken bone.

Definitely not talking to him.

It had nothing to do with the male's creepy, dangerous, air and everything to do with the fact he was obviously a traveller.

Grey needed to speak with a resident if he was going to find out what Archangel had been doing here.

He scoured the small village, trying to spot a local. A few people stopped to stare on their way past. Nothing new there. Grey was used to people staring at him.

He ignored them and continued his search. On the opposite side of the village, two males and a female exited the largest of the thatched huts, laughing with each other, a glow to their cheeks. He breathed deep to catch their scent. Smiled. Alcohol.

Was the hut a sort of tavern?

He crossed the village to it, pretending not to notice the way more people stared at him, their eyes tracking his progress. He didn't care. He really didn't.

He bared his fangs at one male, a reaction he hadn't been able to hold back. The male bared fangs right back at him, his pupils turning elliptical in the centre of his red irises.

A vampire.

Grey supposed Hell was probably fabulous in their eyes. No sunshine to make them go crispy. Just endless night.

He flashed fangs at the male again, and stood a little taller as the male turned away and walked in the opposite direction to him. Easy win. Which was strange. Normally vampires liked to fight to claim top spot, to prove themselves the most powerful things with fangs out there. Which was utter bullshit.

Dragons had to be the most powerful things with fangs.

Maybe demons cut a close second, possibly a joint placing with the elves. Grey had heard all manner of things about elves, some of which made them sound dangerous and not as magical and wonderful as he had believed as a kid.

Hellcats slotted in below them.

Vampires barely ranked above the other feline shifters.

Still, it was odd of the male to leave without a fight.

Grey slowed his steps and watched the male walking away. He didn't stop at the perimeter of the village. He kept walking, heading into the darkness, going south-east.

High, bubbling laughter broke the silence.

He shook off his curiosity about the male and returned his focus to his mission, shifting his gaze back to the hut that was possibly a tavern.

Another female toppled out of it, a male following close behind her.

"Excuse me." Grey raised his hand to snag their attention.

Both of them stared blankly at him.

They looked at each other.

Spoke.

In a language he didn't know.

The female was rather animated as she prattled on, tossing her blonde hair over her bare shoulders, revealing a small top that was more strapless bra than corset. Matching black leather hugged her long legs. She was pretty too, a bright glow around her pupils that might have fooled him into believing her a shifter like him.

Only she smelled of sex and sin.

A succubus.

Her partner stood behind her, giving Grey a death glare turned up to the max.

Succubus sidled towards Grey, a wicked sway to her curvy hips and a smile tugging at her cherry red lips.

Crimson bled into the male's eyes, his pupils stretching thin in their centres.

Another vampire.

And this one looked as if he might fight to prove who was stronger.

Grey held his hands up again and shook his head. "My mistake."

He hurried past the male, ducking into the hut. It was cramped inside and he had to remain bent over to avoid banging his head. With all the demons, dragons and elves in Hell, he would have thought someone would have had the foresight to build the walls higher so the roof trusses didn't pose a risk of injury.

He was barely pushing six-five and it was a struggle to reach the bar without knocking a few braincells out, or himself out with them. He didn't want to see a demon pushing seven foot trying to move around in the cramped suffocating space.

Wooden torches rested in metal sconces spaced around the walls and clustered behind the bar area opposite him. Their flames flickered wildly, casting shadows over the males and females seated around the tables that lined the edges of the room. As if it wasn't hot enough already. He huffed and tugged at his damp t-shirt, trying to fan himself a little as the temperature rose. Still, it was nice seeing a colour other than endless black, and having light in his life again.

He found a spot at the black stone bar, squatted there and tried to get the attention of the female serving. A very ample female. Her long mahogany corset pressed her curves inwards, and upwards, and tan leather encased powerful thighs. She poured a drink from one of the five huge wooden barrels stacked like a pyramid behind the bar and then turned back to the customer and set the clay mug down in front of him.

Her eyes glowed as she spoke with the male, a pretty shade of blue with violet hints.

Another succubus.

Was this entire village made up of them?

She brushed her fingers across the male's jaw, and he visibly shuddered and sagged a little, his cheeks turning deep pink as he stared dazedly at her.

Another beautiful and buxom female came to him and ushered him away, out of the door and into the darkness.

The bartender finally noticed him.

Her smile lit up the room and her eyes glowed a little brighter.

Grey cleared his throat and schooled his features, his lips settling in a firm line and his silver eyebrows meeting hard above his blue eyes.

"I just want information."

She looked disappointed.

Possibly confused.

The escorts Thorne had offered were looking more and more like they would have been a fantastic idea.

The brunette blinked and leaned against the bar, her breasts threatening to spill out of her tight corset. She reached for him.

He shook his head. "Just information."

He wasn't interested in anything else. He shut out the mocking voices in his head. It was his choice. He was the one uninterested in her, not the other way around.

"Infor… mace…" A little wrinkle formed between her brightly coloured eyes.

"Information." He pulled his pack off his back, unzipped the main compartment and fished out the papers he had brought with him. He set them down on the stone slab and pointed to the name of the village. "Is this here?"

She stared at the word.

Dammit. Thorne had warned him that the ragtag groups that called this area their home had probably never left Hell so were unlikely to know the mortal tongues.

Someone peered over his shoulder.

A black clawed finger landed on the piece of paper in front of him, close to his. "Here."

Grey jumped and growled at the male beside him. The warlock. Wizard. Whatever the hell he wanted to be called. He reeked of magic and death.

Even the succubus backed off, her usual bright smile and sultry air turning cold and dark. She said something, and the male said something back at her, a bite in his tone.

"You speak English?" Grey didn't want to talk to the male, but he wasn't going to get anywhere speaking with the bartender or anyone else in the joint.

The male didn't nod.

Not a good sign.

"This is here?" He pointed to the name on the piece of paper again.

The male nodded and looked around. "Here."

It was a start.

"You speak her tongue?" Grey pointed towards the bartender. "Speak. Her."

The male frowned, his icy green eyes darkening a shade, and looked at the female, and then back at him. "Yes."

Getting there.

But the male didn't really understand him. He couldn't ask complicated questions and have him relay them to the bartender for her to answer, and the male wouldn't know the answer to them himself since he was clearly just passing through and using the village as a rest stop.

He needed to boil it down into something the male might understand.

"Mortals. Humans." It was worth a shot. He pointed to himself. "I'm looking for mortals."

The male's eyes lit up. He pointed east. "Mortals."

Grey looked in that direction. East. The dragon realm and the Devil's lands were east of here. He slid his blue gaze back to the male, his hackles rising and his animal side growing restless, prowling beneath his skin.

Was the male telling him the truth?

"Mortals?" Grey pointed east, along the length of the bar.

The male nodded and attempted a smile. It came off twisted and disturbing rather than reassuring.

"Definitely?" Because he was starting to get the feeling that the male was trying to get him killed. "Because dragons are that way."

The male shook his head. "No dragons. Mortals."

Grey pulled the map out of his trouser pocket, spread it across the bar top and jammed a finger against the area Sable had labelled as 'here be dragons' and had drawn what he imagined was meant to be a dragon, but it looked more like a snake fighting a spider.

"Dragons." He tapped the paper.

The warlock shook his head again, his eyes darkening another shade and his thin lips flattening. He jabbed a black claw against a spot west of the dragons, and east of their current location.

"Mortals. There."

So close?

Was it possible?

"Here?" Grey pointed to the map.

The male looked as if he was going to kill him if he asked again, an inky sort of darkness growing around his pupils to devour the pale green of his irises.

"Okay. Here it is. Got it. Thanks." Grey bundled up his papers and his backpack in his arms and left before the male could even think about muttering a spell to flay his fur off his body.

9

He breathed deep as he hit the village square again, shaking off his nerves and the sensation that the male was trying to get him killed. He just smelled of death, that was all it was. It had put Grey on edge.

He looked back at the tavern. Even the succubi had avoided the male. He turned away from the village and headed east, glancing at the male's tent as he passed it. It was set up a good distance from the rest of the tents and from the huts, placed right against the perimeter wall of the village.

That struck a chord in him.

The warlock had come to the village, but had separated himself from them, was keeping his distance even though he obviously wanted to be around others.

The male had been helpful, but because he had looked different to the others, Grey had found it difficult to trust him. He had judged him on his appearance, and had believed he wanted to kill him because of that. He was no better than the others.

He should have been.

Experience should have taught him something, should have made him react differently to the male, but he had treated him with suspicion, just like the rest.

Just like his pride had treated him.

All because he was different to them.

Gods, he was no better than them.

He hated that.

It weighed him down as he trekked east, following the lead the male had given him.

It took him across the valley basin to the foot of a low mountain range.

He looked along it in both directions, and then at his map. By his calculations, the quickest route would be over the mountains, because the range stretched in both directions for miles. If he tried to go around, it would take him at least another day to reach the destination the warlock had marked for him.

By then, Archangel might have moved on.

He adjusted his pack on his shoulders, huffed and started forwards, picking a path up the gently sloping side of the mountain. He crossed a trail around two hundred metres up and followed it as it wound through the sharp towering rocks and up through tall crevasses that sliced into the black mountain. The trail grew narrow near the top, heading towards a sweeping curve between two peaks.

He brought his pack around to his front and pressed his back against the black rock as he edged sideways along the path, his eyes on the steep drop to jagged rocks below and his heart hammering against his ribs. No damn way he was going to fall. He breathed through the fear, refusing to let it get to him, and looked to his right, focusing on the path instead.

It opened up a short distance ahead.

Relief was quick to sweep through him when his boots hit the wider path and the trail led away from the edge, over the ridge.

Gods, he was tired.

He pulled a cloth from his back pocket and wiped the sweat from his brow, and ran his other hand over his silver hair. He would rest on the other side. This high up the mountain, he was unlikely to run into any wild beasts. He could spare a few minutes to catch his breath and rest his legs. He unhooked the canteen from his pack, took a swig of the tepid water, and capped it and put it back again. He was getting low.

Thorne had warned him not to trust the water in Hell.

Apparently, some of it wasn't water at all.

Grey didn't want to know what that meant.

He figured it wouldn't end well for him and that was enough to have him steering clear of hitting any stream he saw for a refill of his canteen.

He reached the top of the mountain.

His breath caught.

Good gods.

It was as if he could see the entire world.

Or at least all of Hell.

Beyond the valley far below him, steeper mountains rose, forming ridge after ridge into the distance, where the sky glowed bright gold. The Devil's domain.

Hell was bleak, grim, but had a strange sort of beauty to it from up here.

He started down the mountain, his eyes leaping back to the view whenever they could, drinking it in. It was incredible. How big was Hell? He should have looked back in the other direction at the ridge to see if he could figure it out. Maybe he would stop there and drink it all in if he came back this way.

He picked out a spot to rest as he scouted the route ahead of him, a nice flat space just a little over halfway down the mountain and only accessible from one side, giving him some protection.

He was close to it when lights in the valley caught his eye.

He slowed his steps and tracked them as they flickered and danced, a row of flaming gold spots crossing the darkness, heading to his left, deeper into the valley.

Archangel?

He looked in the direction they were heading, and frowned. More lights glowed there. Another village? Or a base of operations for a mortal hunter organisation up to no good?

Thoughts of resting scattered and he marched down the mountain, intent on reaching the valley floor before the people walking towards the settlement reached it. He needed to find out if they were Archangel soldiers, and he needed to do it before they joined up with the others. He could handle a few hunters, but not an entire base of operations.

His boots skidded on the loose black shale as he hurried down the mountain, and he fought for balance more than once, attempting a controlled slide that would get him down into the valley quicker than using the paths.

When he hit the valley floor, he paused for breath, his eyes scanning the dimly lit world around him. He spotted the torches off to his left, about five hundred metres out from his current position. He drew down a deep breath, held it in his lungs to steady his heart and centre himself and exhaled slowly. His senses sharpened, his animal side rising to the fore, allowing him to see into the darkness ahead of him.

Allowing him to see the people crossing the valley.

Every inch of him stilled.

And then a slow burn started in his blood.

It wasn't Archangel.

He growled low in his throat at the sight of the large male figures, at the thick chains they gripped, and the captives they dragged along behind them.

It was slave traders.

He caught a flash of the two tiger shifter females he had found huddled naked and terrified in their cages, held against their will by Pyotr, the male Maya had been promised to as a cub.

That burn grew hotter, fiercer, blazing white hot, and he curled his hands into fists, his emerging claws digging into his palms as his tiger side raged, battered his control and pushed him to react, to obey his instincts.

To protect.

No one deserved to be treated that way. No one deserved to be abused, mistreated, held captive and condemned to a life of fear.

He snarled through his fangs.

Dumped his backpack and stripped off his t-shirt.

These bastards were going to pay for what they were doing.

CHAPTER 2

It was almost her turn on the stage.

Sickness brewed in Lyra's stomach and her legs trembled beneath her weight, but she refused to let fear overcome her. She tugged at the heavy metal collar around her neck, rattling the chain attached to it, and cursed. Her heart thundered at a dizzying pace that made it difficult to breathe.

Gods.

She needed to get away.

It was pointless though. There was a huge gulf between what she needed and what she knew was going to happen. She needed to be realistic, and not allow her fear to consume her. She had to keep her head.

Even if she did manage to get the collar off, and the shackles that bound her wrists, she wouldn't be free. She would still be locked in a cage built of the strongest metal in Hell.

Lyra paced the small space, struggling to breathe through the panic as it started to sink its claws into her heart and her mind, conjuring vile images of her future, visions that tore at her strength, making it easier for the fear to take hold.

To strip away her control.

She sucked down another trembling breath.

She needed to be strong.

It was hard when she was falling apart inside.

The number of eyes on her grew, pushing at her fragile restraint, making her want to lash out at the other captives as they watched her.

She hated the sense of expectation that laced the warm air and pressed down on her.

These people expected her to be strong. Fearless.

She might be a hellcat, one of the most powerful and vicious of the shifter species that called Hell their home, but she still had a heart.

She still experienced fear.

The thought of what was about to happen to her was terrifying.

She clawed at her cuffs and her collar, her throat growing tight and her strength wavering for a heartbeat before she snatched hold of it and clung to it again, not letting it bleed from her.

She cursed the collar.

The magic in it sapped her strength, making it impossible for her to break free of her bonds, the drain it caused far stronger and more devastating than the one she felt from the shackles around her wrists. Those were just the back-up plan, a last resort in case she broke her collar somehow. They would inhibit her enough that she wouldn't be able to break them open, but they wouldn't stop her from snapping the chain and gaining enough freedom to sink fangs and claws into every male present.

Everyone responsible for what had happened to her.

She tugged at the ring of cold steel around her neck and growled.

Damn collar.

She let her left hand hang from it, her fingers looped over the top of the ring, and fought for the strength to push back against the feelings welling up inside her, the despair that would allow weakness to invade her heart and her body.

It would break her.

She closed her eyes and cursed again.

Aiming it at herself this time.

Gods, if she hadn't been such a fool, none of this would have happened to her. She would be home, living the life she loved. Her need to track down others of her species had been a moment of weakness, brought on by loneliness, and she should have weathered it as she had every other time it had swept over her. She should have stayed far away from Hell.

Hindsight was a bitch.

She had longed for company, and now she longed for the solitary life she had left behind.

Her moment of weakness had only proven that she was better off alone.

Lesson learned.

Never trust another hellcat.

Lyra tugged at the collar, her strength flowing from her again, despair swift to roll in to take its place, eating away at her.

A collar a male hellcat had placed on her.

She shouldn't have trusted him. Her mother would roll in her grave if she could see her now. Her aunt would roll right along with her. They had raised her better than that. She had been such an idiot, believing herself stronger than both of them, thinking that what had happened to them wouldn't happen to her because she was more intelligent, had learned from their history and seeing the scars that ringed their necks every day of her life.

She had been a damned fool.

All males of her kind were the same.

They wanted to collar any female they met, using it to force them to become their 'mate'. It was the reason most females of her species despised their male counterparts and had long ago decided to do without them, to find their fated ones instead of allowing a male to collar them.

So, the males of her species had grown vicious, driven to dominate the females in response to the rejection, determined to claim what they viewed as rightfully theirs.

She opened her eyes and looked towards the glow that filled the air in the distance to her left, where the stage had been set up and a low hum of chatter drove back the silence of Hell.

Was there a male of her kind in the audience, waiting to bid on her? Eager to have her at his mercy?

Was she about to face the same dark fate as her mother and aunt had?

She shuddered at the thought of any male having that sort of power over her.

Owning her.

"You." The deep voice sent a tremor through her and she whipped her head around and bared her fangs at the huge bare-chested male.

The demon smirked at her, his broken pale horns flaring a little from behind his ears, pushing through his shaggy mane of sandy hair. He always got off on her threatening him. The sick bastard enjoyed taunting her.

The dark-haired demon next to him just stalked forwards, keys jangling in his hands as he searched for the one that would unlock her cage.

Her heart kicked into overdrive again, pulse slamming hard.

She backed away.

Her bottom hit the back of the cage, the metal bars cold against her bare flesh, and she bared her fangs again, hissed through them at the two males, warning them away.

The brunet demon ignored her and unlocked her cage.

The blond flicked his wrist, extending the baton he held. "Be nice now."

He grinned at her, revealing short fangs, a glimmer of arousal in his pale eyes. He wanted her to do the opposite to his words. He wanted her to fight him.

Gods, she wanted it too, but she wasn't about to give the bastard the satisfaction of fighting with her.

A loud roar sent silence sweeping across the black lands.

And a shiver down her spine.

It wasn't one of her kind.

But there was such anger in that roar, such strength and power, and it lit a fuse inside her.

She exploded from the cage, launching at the two males, everything she had held bottled up inside her blasting through her, driving her into a rage.

She was on the brunet demon before he was even aware she had moved, her bare body slamming into his. Her left foot skidded on the loose dirt as she drove forwards, putting all her remaining strength into shoving him backwards and off balance.

As she landed on his chest, the captives in the cages around her began shouting, some of them calling to her to free them while others screamed for the guards, their fear of being punished because of something she had done driving them to alert the bastards who held them in chains in the hope they would avoid a beating.

Lyra sank her claws into the demon's shoulders and struck hard with her fangs, lodging them deep in the side of his throat. He roared and bucked up, but she held on, refusing to release him as he tried to shake her off him. She snarled, a red rage pouring through her, controlling her actions.

She didn't feel it when the sandy-haired demon struck her across the back with his baton. She didn't feel it when he sank his own claws into her arm and pulled. Didn't feel it when the male beneath her managed to shove his fist hard into her stomach.

She felt only the high of battle, the roar of victory in her ears, and the sheer elation that came with the taste of blood on her tongue.

The pale-horned demon finally managed to yank her off his colleague.

To his detriment.

Her fangs ripped through the side of his neck, gouging a deep hole in his flesh. Blood spurted across the black ground, and the male fumbled, desperately seeking the strength to cover the wound. The blond tossed her through the air and she shrieked as she hit the cage, the top bar of it slamming hard into her lower back, sending pain ricocheting through her.

By the time she had hit the ground, the dark-haired demon was still, his eyes staring blankly into the dark beyond.

The blond turned towards her, a growl on his lips.

Lyra roared and sprang at him, hitting him square in the chest with all of her weight. He didn't fall. He grabbed her right arm and spun with her, flung her across the clearing and into the side of another cage. The occupant screamed and shoved at her, pushing her away.

She scowled at the female and spat blood on the floor.

Foolish bitch.

There was no currying favour with their captors now.

Not if the unholy cacophony she could hear coming from the direction of the stage was anything to go by.

Someone was ripping through the crowd, and most likely their captors. Someone who wanted blood on their hands as badly as she did.

She hunkered down and growled low, and the demon backed off as blue flames flickered over her hands.

The need to shift was strong, driving her to obey it, but she couldn't, not with the collar on.

The male knew it. She saw it the moment he remembered, saw all that fear that had been building in his eyes drain right back out of them again as he cockily smiled at her.

Lyra wiped that smile right off his face.

In a lightning fast move, she closed the gap between her and the dead demon, and snatched the baton from his belt. She flicked her right hand out, extending the weapon, and roared as she swept it up in a fast, hard arc aimed at the blond's head.

He growled and dodged backwards, her baton cutting harmlessly through the air a few inches in front of his face.

She strafed left when he swung at her with his own baton, coming close to striking her with it, and threw herself into a roll when he struck again, diving beneath his blow. She came to her feet behind him in a crouch and sprang forwards, leaping high into the air. He turned, a frown on his face as he looked at the ground where she had been.

Lyra grinned as she came down on the bastard's head.

She brought the baton down, a sliver of satisfaction rolling through her when it struck hard enough to crack his skull, and he grunted and dropped to his knees. She kicked off him and pirouetted, coming back around to face him.

He shook his head, his eyes widened as he spotted her baton coming at him again, and he swiftly brought his arm up to shield his face. Another satisfying crack sounded as she connected with his wrist.

How many times had he beaten her with his baton?

How many times had he smiled as he did it, taking satisfaction from hurting her?

Gods, that left her cold. She was no better than he was.

It didn't stop her though. She could hate herself later, when she was free, and this male was dead.

She pressed her left hand against the tip of the baton and drove forwards, into the male's arm, shoving him sideways. He lashed out at her again, his baton striking her thigh and then her knee. Heat swept through her, numb at first but then fiery hot, blazing along her bones.

"Fucker," she snarled and grabbed his baton before he could strike her with it again.

She wrestled with him as he tried to twist it free of her grip, his face contorting into vicious lines as he growled at her, flashing his fangs. His busted horns curled further, a flare of aggression, and his eyes brightened, glowing gold around his pupils.

He yanked his arm backwards, and she went forwards with it, refusing to release his weapon. She slammed into him, her bare breasts pressing against his chest, and pulled her arm back, trying to get the damned baton off him. She was going to kill him with the fucking thing. It would be a fitting end for him. Dying by his own weapon.

She was so focused on getting the baton off him that she didn't notice his other fist coming at her face until it was too late. Pain splintered across her nose and blood poured from it, hot as it ran over her lips. She growled, grabbed his arm and twisted it hard.

He roared as the bone snapped.

Lyra grabbed her baton with both hands, shoved it against the front of his throat and pressed forwards, driving him down into the dirt. She settled all her weight on his chest, her knees pinning his shoulders, and pushed downwards on the baton. His eyes grew wild as he struggled beneath her, kicking his legs and growling.

His baton smacked her hard in the side.

She snarled, grabbed it and twisted it free of his grip.

And brought it down hard.

His eyes widened.

His struggles instantly ceased.

Lyra collapsed to her left, sinking to her backside on the rough black ground, her right leg still draped over the dead demon. She breathed hard, her eyes fixed on the baton sticking out of his chest.

Gods. What had she done?

It wasn't like her.

Her mother and aunt hadn't raised her to be like this.

She lifted her hands and stared at the blue flames that fluttered around her fingers and flickered from her black nails.

She slowly closed her fingers into fists and clenched them. They had driven her to this, and now it was too late to turn back. She needed to keep going.

She needed to make them all pay.

She would show them how vicious a hellcat could be.

She picked herself up, found the ring of keys the demon had used to unlock her cell, and went through them one by one as a battle raged around her, the guards uninterested in her as they rushed either towards the fight at the stage, or ran away into the darkness.

Lucky number thirteen was the one that unlocked her collar.

She pulled it off and let it drop from her hand onto the dirt by the dead demons.

Holy fuck, it felt good.

No more weight around her neck. No more spell sucking all her strength. No more barrier between her and her more powerful form.

She looked for the key to her shackles. None of them were the right sort. Damn. She was going to have to settle for having the collar off for now, at least until she found the son of a bitch who had the key to her cuffs.

The male in charge of the troupe of slavers would be a good place to start looking for it.

After she had killed him.

With the collar gone, she was strong enough to snap the chain between her shackles, giving her more freedom than she'd had in a long time.

She unlocked the cell of the bitch opposite her, and didn't stop to see whether she ran or stayed where she was. She moved on, freeing every prisoner she passed.

A towering male with long matted gold hair and bright gold eyes held his hand out to her.

"Go." He jerked his chin towards the stage.

Towards the fight.

"I have this." His deep voice rolled like thunder over her, filled with darkness and a sensation of danger that had her wanting to take a step backwards, away from him. "I'll set these people free while you deal with them."

She was about to ask whether he was sure he could handle himself if some of the guards attacked him when she finally got his collar open. The second the lock on it popped, he took it and twisted it in his hands, bending the metal as if it was tinfoil.

A flare of bright gold illuminated his eyes.

He held his hand out to her again as he looked down at her with a regal tilt to his chin and an air of authority that warned her not to question him.

Lyra placed the ring of keys into it.

She wasn't about to ask a dragon if he could handle himself.

They tended to take any question about their strength personally and she wasn't interested in becoming barbequed cat.

If he wanted to play the role of white knight, she was more than happy to let him get on with it.

She had a date with someone else.

She nodded at the same time as he did, and then turned and sprinted towards the stage.

Another roar rose above the din of battle, calling to her, driving her to fight.

She growled as she leaped and shifted in mid-air, the transformation swift to come. By the time she landed, it was on four large paws as her twin tails whipped behind her, the blue flames fluttering along the last third of their lengths dancing in the darkness and lighting the area around her.

Cerulean fire burst from beneath her black paws too, and as her anger took hold again, the flames spread up her legs and over her sleek black body. She exhaled hard, causing the flames that licked around her sharp fangs to flutter outwards, and then inhaled, drawing them back.

Her flames were normally warm, a comforting feeling, but in the midst of her rage they were hot, heating her fur, stoking the fire that burned inside her.

She growled and her twin tails swished viciously, the flames that now coated them breaking free and shimmering in the air for a second before they died.

She scanned the area ahead of her, blocking out the sounds of the battle piece by piece as she searched for the one who had put her in the cage. The one who would have sold her into a life of hell.

She snarled, flashing her fangs.

The demon in charge stood on the far side of the dark wooden stage, the huge flaming torches that marked each corner of the platform causing golden light to flicker over his black hair and horns, his matching leathers and his bare chest.

He looked her way, his dark leathery wings twitched against his back and he said something to the three males surrounding him as he pointed at her.

The trio of demons dropped from the stage and started towards her.

Lyra was feeling gracious enough to meet them halfway.

She sprinted across the black dirt, her long legs and preternatural speed devouring the distance in the blink of an eye, and pressed down hard with her back legs once she was close to the demon in the lead.

She sprang, leaping through the air, her claws extending as she arced towards him. The male caught her, twisted and flung her before she could so much as scratch him. She hit the dirt, tumbled and growled as she came onto her paws. She leaped again, and he braced himself, arms open, ready to catch her and toss her again.

Lyra grinned inside as she dropped short of him and launched forwards, her fangs aimed at his thigh. His scream rent the air as she sank them deep through his dark leathers, and warm blood flooded her mouth. Another of the males grabbed her by the scruff and pulled her off him, throwing her into the dirt hard enough to knock the wind from her lungs.

She shook it off before he could attack and lashed out at him, hissing as her ears flattened and flared backwards. He dodged backwards to evade her blow and growled at her, his horns curling as he reached for his baton.

When he flicked his wrist to extend it, the damned thing sparked.

She growled at it and leaped when he tried to hit her with it.

Pain she could withstand to a certain degree, but she had learned early on in her captivity that an electrical charge pouring through her body was something she never wanted to experience again.

He grinned and lashed out again, a bright blue arc following the tip of his baton as it swept towards her.

Lyra leaped again, barely dodging it, and snarled as her back slammed into something.

The male behind her grabbed her and she wrestled against him, flailing madly in his grip, desperation driving her actions as it seized hold of her.

The demon with the baton advanced, and the one she had bitten joined him, extending his own weapon.

No.

"Secure her, or it's our damn heads on the block," the ringleader hollered in the demon tongue, a language she had learned among others during her upbringing.

Her mother had wanted her prepared for anything.

Nothing could have prepared Lyra for this.

She hissed and whimpered as the first baton hit her, sending enough voltage through her body to have her fur standing on end and her flames receding. She growled and struggled against the demon holding her. He tightened his grip. Another baton struck, another thousand volts lighting her up.

She needed to escape. The urge drove her, instinct screaming at her to shift because it would make it easier for her to fight in this situation, but the pain kept her locked in her feline form.

Trapped.

Gods, she would have given anything right that moment to have been any other species of feline shifter. Hers was the only one that shifted into the feline form in response to pain. All the others shifted back to their human one.

The demons struck again, and again, electricity and pain coursing through her, stealing her consciousness and driving her deep into her animal instincts as she tried to withstand the beating and protect her mental state, aware that if she remained lucid, the damage the demons did would be permanent.

A scar on her mind that would last forever.

She howled in agony as one of the demons struck hard on her hind left leg and bone shattered.

Awareness drifted away from her.

She growled at the creatures around her, hungry for the taste of their blood. They meant to kill her. She would kill them first.

She would devour them so their souls could not pass on to their ancestors.

She snarled and twisted, using all her strength against the one holding her. The creature growled but she broke away from it, tipped the fiend off balance and landed on it. She sank her teeth deep into his flesh, tore at it and savaged him with her claws, a blue glow engulfing her. Pain throbbed in her flank, searing her bones. The creature's fault. It would pay for hurting her.

Her fangs found his throat and she ripped at it, feasted on his blood and his screams.

Suddenly he was gone, and the world whizzed past her.

She grunted as she landed on the dirt, on her left leg, sending fresh fire rolling up it that threatened to steal her consciousness from her. Never. She clung to it, refusing to succumb to the darkness, and pushed onto her paws, setting her sights on the next creature.

Both brandished long sticks.

Weapons.

The ones they had struck her with, hurt her with.

She growled at the sticks, instinct driving her to avoid them, to keep away from them. They were pain. They were agony.

They were death.

The two creatures advanced.

Broke apart.

Circled her in two directions.

They were going to attack at once.

She wouldn't stand a chance, but she would at least take one of them with her.

The one on the right was stronger, larger.

She limped backwards, each step agony, sending pain so fierce through her that her vision wobbled and grew dark around the edges.

The one on the left was easier prey.

Blood suddenly spilled down its bare chest from a gash across its neck.

The fiend gargled, hands flailing wildly, the baton forgotten as it fell to the floor, all of its focus locked on trying to stem the blood that flooded like a waterfall over its body.

She stared, struggling to comprehend how the creature had died.

The male dropped to the ground.

Her breath left her in a rush of cerulean flames.

A silver-haired warrior stood where the creature had been, ice-blue eyes bright and naked body streaked with crimson, his claws dripping blood as he held his hand out at his side.

Every instinct she possessed fired at the sight of him.

Male. Warrior.

Mine.

CHAPTER 3

Grey was beginning to think it had been a mistake to let his emotions get the better of him.

Sure, the fight to free the captives held in the procession had been satisfying, and easy.

The few demons that had been leading the slaves across the valley hadn't been difficult to take down in his tiger form, mostly because the first two hadn't seen him coming. The third had tried to run, and the fourth had been too dumbstruck to put up much of a fight.

When they had all breathed their last, he had shifted back and freed the captives, a sense of satisfaction rolling through him.

Until he had stood alone in the valley, and had grown aware of the lights in the distance, of the fact that others were there, locked in chains and fitted with collars.

About to be sold to the highest bidder.

A black rage had come over him, swift to consume him.

He had shifted in a heartbeat, and had been sprinting across the valley in the next, determined to reach the black market and put an end to what was happening.

The moment he had seen the stage and the bastards filling the space in front of it, waving numbers and shouting bids, the moment he had scented the fear of at least a dozen people, all of them different species, he had lost it.

Two guards had met death at his claws and fangs.

A third had hit him hard enough to drive him back out of his tiger form.

Which was never a problem.

He could fight in both forms, had honed his skills over the three centuries he had been alive, all so he could protect his charge, Maya, and his family.

So he could protect the damned pride too, he supposed, although they didn't particularly deserve it.

Or want it.

He pushed thoughts of the pride out of his head as he grappled with a fae male of some kind. He whipped his head forwards, cracking the male's skull with his brow, and the male grunted and staggered backwards, clutching his head. Grey didn't give him a chance to escape, or gather himself. He launched at the male, grabbed his head in both hands, and twisted hard, snapping his neck.

The male dropped lifeless to the floor.

Most of the bastards who had been bidding on the auction had fled, but a few had remained, obviously hungry to make sure they got whatever poor soul they had purchased. One of them was frantically arguing with the demon Grey had figured was in charge, a burly male who stood on the stage, protected by three guards and showing zero inclination to join the fight.

Was he so sure that Grey would meet his end before he reached him?

There were only a handful of enemies between him and the male now.

A sudden surge of people rushing towards him had him growling and hunkering down, preparing for them to attack him. He frowned as they ran straight past him, some of them not stopping while others joined the fight.

Shackles clanked and chains jangled as they attacked the guards that had been on his to-do list.

The slaves.

Someone had freed them.

He looked off to his right, towards the cages he had spotted earlier, and his gaze caught on something as a roar sounded.

Something incredible.

Blue flames lit the darkness around the sleek black-panther-like feline as it faced off against two demons, shimmering over the entire length of its body.

A chill chased over his skin as he stared.

A hellcat.

He had read about them, but he had never seen one.

The closest he had come to seeing one was Maya, and she only had the black nails of a hellcat when she lost her temper. Their mother had told him once that he had the eyes of a hellcat, pure cerulean, like precious gems, and it was the smattering of hellcat blood that remained in him from his ancestor cross-breeding with one that had given him those eyes.

Their mother had been a bit of a romantic.

It wasn't whatever trace of hellcat genes he had that had given him blue eyes.

It was his deformity.

The hellcat edged backwards, away from the two demons with their damned batons.

No.

The hellcat *limped* backwards.

Grey growled and stalked towards the males, fury boiling in his veins, a need to kill them both for sinking so low as to attack an injured hellcat.

A female.

He caught her scent as he neared, and gods, his anger flared hotter in response, his claws emerging and his fangs growing long. A need to shift swept through him, but fear held it back, a feeling he didn't understand as he set his sights on the smaller of the males.

The pain that had forced him out of his tiger form had ceased. He could shift. He was stronger as a tiger.

His gaze flicked to the hellcat.

Cold chased through him at the thought of her seeing him in his feline form.

Abomination.

He growled, and poured all the anger, the rage, he felt on hearing that word chanting in his head in the collective voice of his pride, into his attack. He closed the distance between him and the demon in a heartbeat, had his claws against the bastard's throat in the next second, and had sliced it open on the third.

The male dropped hard as his life flowed out of him, revealing the hellcat. Her eyes met his.

Bright pools of tropical ocean that he wanted to drown in.

He growled, scooped up the baton the demon had dropped, and hurled himself at the second male. The demon blocked his first blow, but the second connected, striking the male hard across his wrist.

Grey struck again, slamming the electric baton into the male's chest point first.

The demon grunted and shuddered as the charge unleashed, pouring into him.

Out of the corner of Grey's eye, the hellcat began inching away from him, dragging her rear left leg.

He couldn't blame her for trying to escape when she saw the chance.

Shackles circled her front legs.

She had been a captive of these males, might have been sold if Grey's temper hadn't got the better of him.

Or the warlock hadn't given him this location as a place to find mortals.

Grey had been an idiot to think the male had meant Archangel soldiers were here.

The male had presumed he wanted a mortal, and had pointed him in the direction of where to get his hands on one. A slave auction. It wouldn't surprise him if the warlock had been on his way to buy a few poor souls for himself. He didn't want to think about what a warlock might want with slaves.

The demon struck him across his right cheek, bringing him back to the fight and reminding him that now wasn't the time to think about things.

It was the time to act.

Grey snarled through his fangs and brutally shoved his baton under the demon's chin and pressed the button to unleash another blast of electricity.

It was enough to send the demon down and have him shaking uncontrollably.

Grey hit him again, a blast right into his temple, and held it there until the bastard stopped shaking and went still.

He picked up the male's baton and twirled them both in his hands.

That left just the son of a bitch in charge of this disgusting auction.

Grey growled when he realised the male was gone.

The whole arena had emptied.

Leaving him alone with the hellcat.

He advanced towards her.

She turned and hissed at him, ears flattening against her head, fangs enormous. Her bright blue eyes warned him away, her flames growing larger, more violent as they danced over her black fur.

They stuttered a second later and she slumped, but was quick to pick herself back up and shake it off.

He dropped the batons to the black dirt, aware that it had been a mistake to keep hold of them when approaching her.

They had made her view him as a threat too.

The pain had her locked deep in her animal side, and that animal associated the batons with pain, and with her enemies, people out to hurt her.

Grey held his hands up at his sides. "I can feel you're afraid."

Which freaked him out a little.

He could sense Maya and Talon's feelings, and Byron's if he bothered to pay any attention to him, but he had always found it hard to get a bead on what others outside of his bloodline were feeling.

She was the first.

Was it just because she was broadcasting her emotions loud and clear to him because her animal was in control, her human mind suppressed by the instinct to survive and the need to shield it from the horror of what had been happening to her?

It had to be, because he didn't want to think about it being anything other than that.

He risked a step closer.

She hissed again and swiped at him, right paw cutting through the air, leaving a trail of blue fire in its wake.

Her flames died down, covering only her paws and the tips of her twin tails, and fluttering around her mouth.

Because she was injured?

He glanced at her hind left leg, taking his eyes off hers for only a second.

In that split-second, she lunged forwards and slashed at him again, but still fell short. She wanted to fight him, feared him as much as she had feared the demons who had beaten her.

"I'm not like them," he whispered and kept his hands held high, hoping she would see he was hardly a threat to her now. He was naked and unarmed. "I'm not going to hurt you... I just want to get you to safety. We can't stay here."

She growled and backed off, placing more distance between them, showing him that she wanted to escape this place as much as he did.

Probably more.

But with her injury, it was slow going. She made it barely three metres in the minute he watched her, and had to keep stopping, her flames dying down each time.

"You're going to pass out if you keep pushing yourself."

She looked back at him and hissed.

Grey sighed. "I get it. You're angry, afraid... but I swear... I am not going to hurt you. I saved you, didn't I? Why would I do that if I was going to hurt you?"

The look she gave him somehow answered him loud and clear.

Because he wanted to put another collar on her.

"Look... I'm not into that sort of thing. I came here to free everyone, not enslave them. I'm not like that." He slowly kept pace with her as she began inching forwards again, stopping every time she did, keeping the distance between them steady. Voices sounded in the distance. She lifted her head and growled, and there was so much pain in it, so much fear in her, that he snapped. "I tried doing this the nice way."

She growled as he closed the gap between them and he ignored her, let her smack him in the legs and try to drive him away.

He felt like a bastard as her fear increased, panic mingling with it in her scent.

She honestly viewed him as a threat.

He bent, grabbed her around her waist, and scooped her up into his arms. She hissed and wriggled, and he grunted as he tried to keep hold of her, which was a damned feat given her size. She was far larger than a tiger, and heavy with muscle that she was doing her damnedest to use against him.

"I can't leave you to fend for yourself and you know people are coming... so you can bite and scratch me all you want, but I'm getting you out of here before they arrive."

She could clearly understand him, but she took the invitation he had issued and raked claws over his shoulders as he twisted her in his arms. He slung her over his shoulder and held her hard over her back, but gently around her hips, aware of her injuries. As much as she obviously wanted to hurt him judging by the war she waged on his back with her claws, leaving fiery trails across his skin and filling the air with the scent of his own blood, he didn't want to hurt her.

He swiftly carried her away from the battleground, heading back towards the mountain range in a direct line. She finally stopped trying to fight him when he reached its base and began to ascend, going still in his arms as he picked his way around boulders and up steep inclines.

For a moment, he feared she had passed out, but her low growls and occasional hisses, and the feelings he could sense in her said that she was still lucid.

Still angry.

He skirted the base of the mountain, his senses fixed as far and wide as he could manage, charting everything.

The people he had sensed drifted into the distance.

Good.

He dropped back down into the valley when he smelled his own scent, and found his backpack and clothes. The moment he put the hellcat down, she growled and tried to get away.

He sighed.

"Really?" He donned his trousers, boots and t-shirt, and then slipped his backpack on over his shoulders.

She got all of a couple of metres from him before he had her back in his arms.

She didn't fight him this time.

He carefully carried her in his arms, which should have been the weirdest thing, cradling a huge feline like a baby, but he had done it once or twice with Maya when she had been younger.

Only this cat was infinitely more dangerous than Maya had ever been.

Blue eyes steadily watched him, pinned to his face as he carried her.

If she wanted, she could easily bite his head off in this position.

He just hoped she got the message that he trusted her.

And she started to trust him in return.

He looked down at her, strange warmth flooding his chest.

That sense of connection returned.

Deeper than before.

He dragged his eyes away from her, fixed them ahead and crushed the feelings she had brought to life inside him.

Whatever she was to him, it wasn't going to happen.

If life had taught him anything, it had taught him this.

No one could ever love him.

CHAPTER 4

A breathtaking silver-haired male stared at her, blue eyes entrancing her and pulling her under his spell, heating her blood to a thousand degrees and flooding her with a single need.

To claim him as her own.

Lyra stared into those eyes, shuttered by dark silver lashes, filled with a thousand secrets and a burning hunger for violence that echoed within her.

He disappeared.

She tracked him as he moved, fluid and graceful, a soul-stealing dance that made every muscle on his bare body come alive. They spoke to her as he fought a demon, lured her deeper under his spell.

She couldn't suppress the low growl of appreciation that rumbled up her throat as she watched him fight, witnessed his raw power and majesty.

Gods.

She wanted to make him belong to her.

She ached for him to stand at her side, the two of them against the world.

A quiet voice whispered in her mind, battling her instincts, gradually rising above them to murmur that this male was dangerous to her and she had to flee. Now was her chance. Everyone was distracted. She had to escape.

She couldn't stay where she was, couldn't allow herself to get swept up in the male.

For all she knew, he was someone from the crowd, a male bent on owning her.

She could not trust him.

The need to leave warred with the need to stay, to remain near this mysterious male.

In the end, leaving won, driving her to limp away.

She looked back over her shoulder at the majestic silver-haired warrior.

He struck the demon down, threw his head back and roared.

Lyra froze.

Her heart pounded wildly.

Blood rushed.

Gods.

He stood in the middle of all the carnage, covered in blood, breathing hard, every carved muscle straining, calling to her.

Drawing her to him.

He dropped his head and his blue eyes met hers, seared her all over again.

Who was this male?

He was the owner of that roar she had heard, the one that had driven her to fight, had unleashed her fury.

A stranger who had wrought a brutal victory and had freed her.

He stalked towards her, setting her heart racing faster, her blood rushing fiercer, and she trembled in response, belly fluttering as she waited.

Waited.

Her breath hitched as he pulled her up into his powerful arms, and his mouth descended on hers, crushing her lips in a hard kiss that claimed a piece of her soul.

Lyra jerked awake and hissed as pain ricocheted up her left leg.

Damn.

She growled as the pain grew fiercer.

"Sorry." The dulcet male voice rolled over her like a warm tide, washing away the pain and giving her something else to focus on.

She hissed again, panic rushing through her as she realised she wasn't dreaming now. She was awake, and she wasn't alone.

The silver-haired warrior was with her.

He crouched beside her, intense blue eyes locked on her left leg as he probed it gently with his fingers, pressing them into her short black fur.

"Shit," he muttered. "It's broken alright."

It didn't take a genius to figure that one out.

He stood, scrubbed a hand over his short tousled hair and sighed, a pensive expression settling on his handsome face.

"Stay put," he said, and then chuckled. "Not as if you're going anywhere. At least you stopped fighting me."

When he turned away, her eyes widened.

Red lines littered his back, crimson trailing from them over his dirty skin, reaching all the way down to the waist of his trousers.

She had done that.

She remembered it now. It was hazy, but there, a flicker of a memory. It was always this way when her animal instincts hijacked her, driving her consciousness deep down. It was a protection mechanism, something all shifters had. Her animal side saw things differently, felt differently, and wasn't as affected by things as her human one. When she was in danger of suffering any sort of mental damage, that animal side took control.

When the male crouched, she followed him, and watched as he tore at the back of his pack. He grunted as he ripped the black material, and tugged out two metal poles. The supports.

When he turned back to her with them, an instinct to survive and protect herself seized her.

She hissed at him, flashing her fangs as her rounded ears twisted backwards and flattened against her head.

He looked down at the two short poles, and then at her, and held his hands up, his eyes wide. "They're not batons. I'm not going to use them to hurt you. I'm just going to use them to fix your leg in place so it can heal, and then you'll be able to shift again."

She fought to suppress the need to fight him as he approached her, cursing her animal side for a change. The male wanted to help her, not hurt her. It was difficult to make herself believe that though, especially when her animal side was still pushing for control, and everything that had happened was still fresh in her mind.

He helped by tucking the two poles down the back of his trousers, out of sight.

The desire to attack him faded.

She watched him carefully as he dropped to his knees beside her. He picked up a t-shirt from the black dirt and ripped it into lengths. She hissed again when he leaned towards her head and draped one of those pieces over her eyes.

"Just don't look," he murmured softly, his voice like honey in her ears, soothing her.

She forced herself to keep still as he took hold of her leg, to deny that urge to fight him and see what he was doing. If she did, her animal side would wrest control from her again the second it saw the poles.

"I'm going to need to align this bone," he whispered. "Gods, I hope you understand me."

He was gentle as he manoeuvred her leg, somehow managing to keep the pain to a dull ache when she had been expecting another blast of white-hot fire.

"I don't know what the fuck I'm doing here... what if I can't do this... maybe the bloody demon was right and I should have taken his men with me... can't speak a damn word that anyone understands in this place."

Lyra had the feeling he wasn't talking to her now. He was talking to himself. Had he been alone so long that he needed to hear someone's voice?

Or was it that he needed to hear a familiar one?

She could understand that desire, because she had talked to herself more than once during her captivity just so she could hear her own voice and take comfort from it, draw strength from it that she had badly needed.

She focused on him, on his accent that sounded British to her ears.

He was a long way from home.

It struck a chord in her.

She was a long way from home too. She didn't belong in Hell. It had been a mistake to come here. It had been a mistake to trust a male of her kind.

"Done." He removed the cloth from her eyes.

She immediately rolled so her front legs stretched before her and her front half was upright. Her left hind leg throbbed. She looked at it, twisted and licked the area around the black bandages, careful not to disturb them but unable to deny her instinct to clean the wound.

"It'll heal faster now," he said and sat on the other side of the small cave to her. "Sorry I can't light a fire. It might attract attention."

She didn't need light to see him. Her vision was sharp enough to make out every detail about him.

He reached into his pack and pulled out another t-shirt.

He didn't put it on.

He moved onto his knees and held it out to her. "I can put it over you if you're cold."

She bared her fangs at him and curled up as best she could with her left rear leg throbbing like mad.

"Message received very loud and clear." He sank back against his side of the cave.

Lyra studied him, using him to block out the pain in her flank.

He was fascinating.

He pulled out a wrapped bar of something from his pack and ate it while keeping an eye on the cave entrance.

"Are there a lot of slavers around here?" He glanced at her and she hissed at his question, just the mention of slavers enough to have her hackles rising. His blue eyes slid her way again. "I'm going to take that as a yes. It never struck me as a particularly nice part of Hell. Apparently, there are nice parts… like the elf kingdom. Have you been there?"

He was at it again, talking to himself, filling the cave with the sound of his own voice.

"I bet they have clean water." He lifted his canteen, shook it and frowned. It sounded almost empty to her. "Is there clean water around here?"

She didn't have an answer to that question.

She didn't really know this part of Hell.

But she knew the realm better than he did.

It struck her again that he was lonely, out of place.

And he was new to Hell.

He swigged his water, recapped the canteen and set it back down, and then stared at the mouth of the cave so long that sleep almost claimed her. It was certainly sneaking up on him. His eyelids dropped and flicked open, and dropped again. He jerked his head up and shook it, and then rubbed his eyes as he yawned. It kept him awake for a few more minutes.

His eyelids grew heavy again.

Before he nodded off, he quietly murmured, "Wake me if you need me for anything… anything at all."

Fascinating male.

She wanted to know his story.

But she wanted to run from him at the same time.

Lyra shut out that desire and focused on him. He had helped her. It was hard for her to trust him though, to see him without part of her remembering how she had trusted a male before, and had ended up sold into slavery.

By one of her own kind.

She hoped the bastard was dead.

She had discovered in one of his enlightening little talks with her, the ones where he sat by her cage and boasted about the things he had done, that it was a trade of his to lure hellcats and sell them on the black market.

Would her mysterious warrior do such a thing?

Was she a potential payday to him?

She fought the lure of sleep just as he had, but she wasn't strong enough to deny it, and she slipped into nightmares about the male who had sold her, the things she had seen and the things they had done to her. Each image fluttered by quickly but left their mark, a cut that was deep and bled, stole her strength and had her desperate to wake again, to escape the horror. She saw her bare dirty feet as they marched her across the wastelands, humiliated and shackled, stripped of her strength.

In a collar.

The sound of metal on metal had her snapping awake.

"Sorry," the silver-haired male muttered and eased back. "I didn't mean to wake you."

There was a touch of colour on his cheeks.

Lyra gasped as she realised she had shifted back.

Panic lanced her and she shot up into a sitting position, hands racing to cover her nudity. They hit soft material where bare flesh should have been.

She looked down at the black t-shirt draped over her body, concealing her curves, and then up at him as she clutched the material to her, touched by what he had done for her.

He diligently kept his eyes off her, fixed on his work.

He hissed through his teeth and muttered something as he tried to pick something up off a small fire, fingers touching the metal cup and then leaping away from it. He eventually managed to hold it long enough to get it off the fire and onto the floor of the cave.

Lyra tried not to stare as he licked the pads of his fingers and then blew on them to soothe them.

He lifted those stunning pale blue eyes to meet hers.

She tensed when he moved onto his knees, closing the distance between them. His black fatigues stretched tight over muscled thighs, and his torso tensed as he rested his hands on those thighs, close to his hips. The blood that had been all over him when she had fallen asleep was gone, scrubbed off every delicious honed muscle on his chest and his arms, leaving golden skin behind.

She saw him as he had been on the battlefield, a warrior naked and covered in the blood of his enemies.

A wild and dangerous male.

He averted his eyes, as if he knew her thoughts and they unnerved him for some reason.

Perhaps it was more that he had felt something in her, that strange and powerful pull she felt towards him, that she couldn't escape. It was like gravity. No matter how fiercely she fought it, it refused to release her.

But she had to be strong. She had to keep resisting.

Because she wasn't sure whether she could trust this male.

She wasn't sure she would ever trust a male again.

It was better she didn't fall under his spell. It was safer.

So no matter what happened, no matter how entrancing he was or how fiercely he tried to bewitch her, she wasn't going to let it sway her.

When she could, she would leave, and she would never see him again.

It was safer.

That way, he wouldn't have a chance to hurt her.

He poured the contents of the metal cup into a plastic one and offered it to her. She stared at it, watching the steam rise lazily from the surface of its contents.

"It's just soup," he said when she made no move to take it. "I used the last of my water to make it. You need to eat."

Damn him for being so thoughtful and kind. He was going to make this hard for her, wasn't he? He was going to push her to her limit and test her, to see if she could keep her distance from him. He was going to try to win her trust.

It wasn't going to be easy.

She took the cup and sipped the soup, but not because he had used the last of his water to make it for her or had been thoughtful enough to give her food.

She sipped it because she needed to regain her strength so she could leave him.

His eyes remained locked on her and he didn't move back to his side of the cave. He remained kneeling in front of her, too close for comfort, so close she could feel his heat and smell his alluring scent of woods and rivers, of pure and clean nature.

She was about to ask what his problem was when he spoke.

"What's your name?"

Fear swept through her.

She wasn't fae, and giving him her name wouldn't give him power over her, but it felt as if it might.

She wanted to keep that barrier between them, needed to hold him at a distance.

Yet she was powerless to stop herself from being drawn towards him.

She was powerless to stop herself from surrendering it to him.

CHAPTER 5

"Lyra."

Grey stared at the slender black-haired female, right into those luminous cerulean eyes.

Gods, she had a beautiful name to match her beautiful looks. He should have expected it, but it hit him hard, would have knocked him on his arse if he hadn't already been sitting.

He looked at the small fire he had risked making so he could heat some soup for her, and then at his knees, anywhere but at her. He had stared at her enough already. If he kept on staring at her, she was going to start feeling nervous, and he didn't want that.

He lifted his eyes back to meet hers. "You were out a while. I took your brace off while you were sleeping."

"How long?" She frowned at her cup and turned it in her hands, and hell, it was sweet relief to know she understood English.

She spoke it with a confidence that said she more than understood it. She was as fluent in it as he was. Although, her accent wasn't British like his. It was hard to place. An accent of Hell?

"Two days... I think." He raised his hands from his knees and turned them, trying to get her to look at his wrists, which felt like a dick move when she ended up looking at her own instead, and the cold metal that circled them. "I don't have a watch... if I'm honest, I don't have a clue what day it is, let alone what time."

She didn't smile at that attempt to lighten the atmosphere.

She remained cold. Distant.

He could understand that though.

She had been through a lot, more than he had guessed if the pronounced scars around her throat and the ones he had seen on her back were anything to go by.

"Drink up," he said and moved back to the other side of the cave to give her some space.

She tucked her legs up against her bottom to keep herself covered. She looked small like that. Fragile. She was strong, he could sense it in her, but there was a frailty to her that called to him, had him wanting to be close to her at all times, roused a need to make her feel safe and protect her.

He forced himself to remain where he was, at a distance from her, and rifled through his backpack, looking for a protein bar or something to keep him going, something to do other than stare at her.

She awkwardly sipped her soup.

The silence in the cave weighed down on him, growing more strained by the second.

He tried to think of something to say to set her at ease and reassure her that he wasn't out to do anything sinister to her.

"It's good," she whispered, shattering the silence for him.

She looked over the rim of her cup at him, her blue eyes instantly pulling his to them. There was something magical about those eyes of hers. Once his met them, he couldn't stop looking into them, found it hard to break free.

If he was being honest, he didn't want to break free of them. He wanted to look into them forever.

"I can't take the credit for that. It came out of a pack." He shrugged and forgot about looking for something to eat and settled for drinking his fill of her instead. "It was my emergency rations."

"You were expecting things to go badly?" Her fine black eyebrows pinched above those alluring pools of tropical blue.

He rolled his shoulders again. "Maybe. It always pays to be prepared."

"Were you in the SAS or something?" Her soft rosy lips almost tilted into a smile.

He smiled at her. "No. Just raised that way."

Gods, this easy banter felt good. When was the last time he had been able to speak with someone like this, someone who wasn't his family?

"Not around here though." She set the cup down beside her knees.

He smiled wider. "That obvious, huh?"

Was she local? He wanted to ask, but he didn't want to push her too hard. He had never heard of a hellcat living in the mortal world, so she had to be local.

She looked as if she wanted to ask him something else, but then she lifted her cup and sipped the soup again, and looked for all the world as if she was hiding in it, avoiding him now.

That dreadful silence descended again.

Cut only by the sound of the broken chains attached to the thick silver cuffs around her wrists jangling as she moved.

Grey glared at them, a need to get them off her flooding him, driving him to do something, even when he couldn't.

He had tried to break them when she had passed out.

Whatever metal they were made from, it was tough, strong enough to withstand all his attempts to remove them. But then, he had been trying to be gentle with her, afraid of waking her with what he was doing. Maybe if he made another attempt now that she was conscious and he had no fear of waking her, he would be able to break them.

She looked down at them. "I couldn't find the key for them. I found the one for my collar."

Collar.

His eyes snapped up to her throat. Settled on the scars that ringed it.

36

Gods.

The thought of her collared had his blood running hot, a fierce inferno sweeping through his veins, and it birthed a dark and terrible need to return to the area where she had been held, where some sick son of a bitch had set up a stage to sell her into slavery, and track down every single person associated with that twisted business.

He wanted to hunt them.

Needed it.

"What's your name?" Her soft voice lured him up from his black thoughts, broke them apart to allow light to shine through.

She wasn't there now.

She was here, safe and free.

With him.

She gave him an expectant look, those blue eyes pulling him back under her spell, making him forget what she had asked.

What was it about this bewitching, beautiful hellcat that had him so on edge around her, torn between a need to move closer to her and a need to distance himself?

"You do have a name?" She canted her head, causing her messy black hair to brush her dirty cheek.

Name.

Yes. He had one.

Hadn't he told her it already?

Fuck, maybe he hadn't. He had been so caught up in hers, and how it fitted her so beautifully, that he had forgotten to repay her courtesy by offering his own.

"Grey," he said.

Husked if he was being honest.

It had come out murmured and intense, filled with emotion he didn't quite understand but he knew was dangerous.

A touch of colour rose onto her cheeks as she looked down at her soup.

It was gone a second later, her pretty face shifting to a blankness that he found he didn't like, because he didn't want her to hide her feelings from him.

She set the cup down.

Didn't look at him.

"Thanks for the soup, but I need to be going now."

Those words left him cold.

She couldn't go.

He had only just found her.

She reached her right hand up above her to grip the black wall of the cave, plastered his t-shirt to her curves with her left arm, and pulled herself up.

Her left leg buckled beneath her.

Grey was across the short distance between them in the blink of an eye and had caught her before she hit the ground.

"That was stupid," he muttered, fury pounding in his veins at the thought she had been so desperate to get away from him that she had hurt herself, a darkness he liked as much as the thought of her leaving.

They mingled together, blurred and had a need flaring inside him, one that demanded he make her stay.

He eased her back down, trying to ignore how the feel of her soft bare skin against his lit him up inside.

She pressed warm palms against his bare chest and shoved hard as she growled and snarled at him, flashing her short fangs.

Grey pushed back against the instincts that gripped him, the ones that told him to exert his strength on her, to bend her to his will and make her submit to him.

It took all of his willpower, but he managed to force himself to release her, the fear he could feel flowing through her giving him the strength to go through with it, because he didn't want to hurt her.

He didn't want to frighten her.

He rose to his feet and took a step backwards, and then pushed himself to take another, and then a third and fourth, until his back was plastered against the rough wall of the cave and he was as far from her as he could get.

It was hard.

Gods, it was hard to stand at such a distance from her when his animal side roared with need the depth of which he had never experienced before.

It shook him.

He pressed his palms against the sharp rocks behind him and clawed at them, focused on the pain to ground himself and on her.

She shook as she clawed at her meagre cover of his black t-shirt, hands trembling violently as she desperately tried to keep herself covered, her heart a wild erratic thundering in his ears.

The urge to hunt and kill those responsible for her mental anguish returned full force, had him looking towards the mouth of the cave to his right and battling the powerful need to leave, to risk losing her in order to avenge her.

But, holy hell, he wasn't sure he would be able to go on living if he returned to find her gone.

Grey closed his eyes, ground his molars together, and clenched his hands into fists that shook as he tried to tamp down the conflicting needs that were pulling him apart, and that terrifying urge to stake a claim on her.

She stilled on his senses, her eyes searing his bare chest, but her heartbeat was off the scale and the scent of her fear grew stronger.

Because he was frightening her, standing there fighting with himself, no doubt giving her the impression he wanted to do something to her that they would both regret.

He didn't. He wouldn't. He was stronger than that, and he would master this need that burned inside him, this hunger that raged out of control.

Because it frightened him too.

It wasn't him.

Gods, what terrible beast had she awoken in him?

He sharply turned away from her, sank to his knees beside his pack and rifled through its contents, pulling his shit together as he did so, slowly shutting down his feelings one by one and mastering them, bringing them back under control. As he worked on finding her something to wear, focusing on the small task of making her feel more comfortable, the hunger began to abate and finally it weakened enough that he could reclaim control.

His hands stopped shaking.

He pulled out an item of clothing, his only spare, and offered it to her without looking at her.

She snatched it from his hand.

Grey averted his face, turning it towards his right, and kept his eyes closed, ignoring that whispered voice that told him to peek at her. That wasn't him. He wasn't that sort of male. The voice grew louder, telling him that she belonged to him now, she just didn't know it yet and he needed to make her know it.

He needed to make her submit.

He ground his teeth again, clenching his jaw so hard they creaked under the pressure.

It wasn't him.

"Shorts?" She sounded horrified, but her voice was still a sweet balm to his aching heart, soothed that part of himself he was finding hard to control, a new and terrifying part that had never existed before he had set eyes on her.

He shrugged as casually as he could manage. "I figured Hell might be a bit warm for my taste."

She huffed, and he was glad to hear and to feel that she was calming again, becoming more at ease around him.

"Done."

He wanted to look at her, but at the same time he didn't, because he wasn't sure he was strong enough to fight the strange urges that came over him whenever he so much as glanced at her.

They troubled him.

They had come on so quickly, strong and fierce, gripping him hard the second she had announced she was leaving.

Had there always been this darker side of himself inside him? Did it come from the fact he had spent his entire life alone, even when he had been surrounded by people? Was it because he had been shunned at every turn, treated with contempt by the very people he had fought to protect?

Or was it something about her that had him feeling this way?

He risked a glance at her.

She sat by the small fire, the warm glow playing across the subtle curves of her face and brightening her eyes as she fidgeted with the belt on the black cargo shorts, trying to tie it tighter around her slender waist.

Gods, he had thought her beautiful as a hellcat, but she had stolen his breath and roused something fierce inside him when she had shifted back and he had seen how much more beautiful she was in her human form.

That something had only grown fiercer as she had spoken to him, passed time with him, told him a little about her past and revealed small details about herself without saying a word.

She lifted those striking blue eyes to meet his and then quickly dropped them again, a touch of innocence about the way she did it that had his heart pounding harder, blood rushing faster.

And that need rising again.

He tamped it back down, refusing to let it control him.

He wasn't like that. He wasn't the sort of male that could force a female to like him.

He stared at her hands, trying to focus on something other than her face to give himself a moment to pull himself back together.

It was a mistake.

Her black nails captured his attention and stirred wicked thoughts. They were long and sharp, made for raking down his back.

He swallowed hard.

This wasn't him.

He was a male made for protecting others, and he would be that male with her.

He would protect her from himself.

"I can get you to the nearest portal." Those words sounded hollow in his ears and his tiger side rebelled against them, snarled and snapped, paced in his heart and filled it with an urge to do the opposite, to keep Lyra here with him instead of setting her loose.

He would protect her in the only way he could.

He would take her to the nearest portal.

And he would never see her again.

CHAPTER 6

Grey was quiet. Too quiet.

He hadn't struck Lyra as the talkative type, more the silent and brooding one, but he had at least said a few words to her, letting her see beyond the façade he maintained so well—the one that made it hard for her to get a clear picture of him.

He had frightened her in the cave when he had gone as still as a statue, clearly battling with himself about something. She had felt things about him loud and clear then, picking up a need in him that ran deep.

A need that was about her.

For a moment, a brief flash of time, she had thought he would succumb to it, but then he had given her clothes and surprised her by giving her as much privacy as he could rather than taking her dressing as a chance to look at her body. By the time she had donned the oversized shorts and t-shirt, he had been a different male, whatever urges that had come over him erased and gone.

Or at least suppressed.

Since they had left the cave over an hour ago, he hadn't said a word.

Whenever she failed to contain a gasp or sharp intake of breath when her leg ached, he would glance at her, his ice-blue eyes asking whether she was alright, but he wouldn't say a word. As soon as he saw she was fine, he went back to staring straight ahead, leading the way over the mountain.

He helped her from time to time, pulling her up steep rocks or assisting her down tricky sections of the narrow path where she might fall because of her leg.

Silent all the time.

Hell, it bothered her.

It shouldn't, but for some reason, it did.

It struck her that she wanted to hear him speak, needed to be able to speak with him in return, because she was beginning to feel as if she was marching again, chained in a line with the other slaves. No one had said a word then, not even the bastards in charge of the procession. Every march had been done in silence, only the jangling chains breaking the quiet.

Like the chains that dangled from her heavy cuffs and clinked with each step she took.

Her throat tightened.

Pulse accelerated.

She stopped and squeezed her eyes shut against the onslaught of images, memories of the marches that blurred together, and then the cages, locked in them every time the group had rested at one of the camps.

She swallowed hard, lowered her head and clenched her fingers into tight trembling fists at her sides.

She wasn't there now.

She wasn't marching with other slaves, she was striding towards her freedom.

No. She was already free.

"Lyra?" Grey whispered, and she became aware of how close he was to her, his warmth surrounding her and that soothing but enticing scent of woods and earth, and summer rain filling her senses.

She shook her head, but she couldn't find her voice to tell him that she was fine and he didn't have to worry about her.

She felt the air shift, felt his need to touch her shoulder and his hand coming close to her, and then he stepped back instead, leaving her strangely cold inside and aching for him to have chosen the other route, the one where he would have placed his strong, large hand on her and held her.

Damn, this whole situation had messed her up.

She didn't need a male. She didn't want one. She certainly couldn't bring herself to trust one again after what had happened to her.

Could she?

She opened her eyes and slowly lifted her head, skimming her gaze over Grey's heavy black leather boots, up those long powerful legs encased in black fatigues, and across the delicious and tempting display of tight eight-pack abdominals and the broad slabs of his pectorals, to the strong line of his neck and his handsome face, with enticing full lips and those entrancing blue eyes.

Gods, she wanted to trust him.

But she couldn't.

She didn't need a male.

She had finally learned the lesson her mother and aunt had tried to teach her, first-hand experience driving it home that she couldn't trust males. They wanted to subjugate her kind, wanted to turn her into a breeder for them, a slave to their every whim.

That wasn't the life for her.

She was happy with the one she had forged for herself in her mountain home, far from the heat of Hell, a solitary existence that suited her and she loved.

"I'm fine now," she murmured, lost in those glacial blue eyes that reminded her so much of home. "I just… the quiet… the walking… it made me think of… back then… when I was… caught… and whenever we moved location."

His handsome face darkened, a storm gathering in his eyes, causing them to glow bright blue around his pupils, and then he drew down a slow breath and exhaled, and somehow pushed out all of the darkness with it.

Or pushed it all down inside him where it would continue to build until it became too much for him to contain.

"We can talk," he said, and looked off to his left, down the steep path that wove down the side of the mountain to the valley below. He pointed to a place halfway across the valley basin. "It's still a long walk to the village and another day to the portal from there. We can rest at the village… or here… if you're tired."

He struck her as a male who was always aware of others and their needs, and that tugged at the curious side of her.

"The village is fine," she said, mostly because she wanted as much distance as possible between her and the slave camp, and she was aware it was still close, too close for comfort.

He started walking again, adjusting the pack on his back as he traversed a steep section of path.

He had good footing. Was he used to scaling mountains? The way he moved said that he was, and that he had spent a lot of time around mountains and knew the pitfalls to look for and how to move along the paths without causing any landslips.

It struck another chord in her, one that resonated and soothed her, and increased the small part of her that felt she could trust him.

"So, do you often come to Hell on your vacations?" She wasn't sure why she had felt the need to ask him that in such a teasing manner. It was strange, completely the opposite of her usual straightforward manner.

Something about him made her want to tease him though.

Or was it something about her?

She wanted to feel more comfortable around him, and wanted him to feel comfortable around her. She wanted to feel closer to him, and not only because whenever she felt close to him the hell of her captivity felt further away, as if it was already a distant memory.

He laughed.

Sweet gods, it was warm and rich, sent a pleasant hot shiver down her spine and heated her skin.

"No. It's my first time." He glanced over his shoulder at her, the smile that tugged at his lips tugging at a part of her too. "I'm trying to help out my brother."

"You have a brother?"

He nodded. "Two… but I'm not talking to one of them right now. I have a little sister too. Shit, she's all grown up now though, off falling in love and finding her mate. The brother I'm here for, he did the same damn thing. Ran right into his fated one the night he escaped captivity."

She stilled. "He was a captive?"

Grey stopped, turned back to her and nodded again. "Talon is strong though… a little like you. He's shaking it off and getting on with his life now. I think having Sherry in it has helped him a lot… but he saw stuff in the place where he was held and it's bugging him."

"So you said you would look into it for him." She stared at him as he rolled his shoulders in a casual shrug, as if the fact that he had come to Hell, to a place foreign and dangerous to him, for the sake of his brother was nothing.

"Can't let curiosity kill that cat, I'm afraid. He's my brother."

He was more than that. She could see it in his eyes, in the love they held. They had lit up the moment he had started talking about his family. He loved them dearly, even the brother he apparently hated.

He was literally going to Hell and back for one of them.

Grey turned away from her and started walking again. "Since I had nothing keeping me at the pride anymore, I figured I would do a little travelling, and here I am."

It was more than that.

She felt it in his words, in the meaning locked within them, and in him as he moved away from her. He was struggling. He was trying to act casual, to let something roll off his broad shoulders and not affect him, but it was. It was bothering him. Weighing him down.

He had nothing keeping him at the pride anymore.

The truth was, he didn't want to be there.

He figured he would do a little travelling.

He was looking for the place where he wanted to be.

"What was it?" She started after him, limping down the mountain path, not wanting him to get too far away from her all of a sudden.

He looked back over his right shoulder at her. "What was what?"

"The thing your brother was curious about?"

"A door."

She frowned at that. "A door?"

What sort of male was curious about a door?

"More specifically, what they were holding on the other side and why it needed two guards to protect it at all times."

That made more sense. She would be curious about such a door too.

"When Talon's mate broke back into the place with him to help him free the other captives, she found some information and one of the files she downloaded is definitely about the door. I'm following up the leads… but it's harder than I thought it would be. I don't speak the lingo down here, and it turns out not many of Hell's residents speak English. I'm surprised you do."

"I'm not a resident of Hell."

He glanced back at her again. "You're not?"

She shook her head. "I hate it here. I speak good English because I live in Norway."

His silvery eyebrows rose. "Fancy that. So what brought you to Hell?"

"Idiocy. But we were talking about you. It must run in your blood." When he gave her a quizzical look, she added, "The penchant for risking your neck to free captives."

A hint of a smile touched his lips, but lasted only a second. "I just… with what happened to Talon, and then my sister Maya almost ending up a slave of some fucker that she had been promised to at birth… I just snapped when I saw the people in chains marching towards their doom."

"There aren't many in this world who would risk their life in order to free slaves they didn't even know and would never see again… people who probably wouldn't even thank them." She was sure most people in the world would look in the other direction and just walk away.

Grey had done something about it instead.

He tried to shrug again, but it was stiff this time. "Some thanked me… I think… like I said, I don't speak the languages down here."

Lyra stepped towards him, narrowing the distance between them, and held his gaze. "Thank you, Grey."

Rose coloured his cheeks and he looked away from her. "It was nothing."

It was something.

Not only had he freed her, but he had carried her kicking and snarling away from that terrible place, and had tended to her wounds.

She had never met a male with a heart as big as his one.

He had saved her, and scores of other slaves. He had come to Hell to help his brother, and even though he didn't speak the languages of this realm, he showed no sign of giving in and going home.

Oh hell, she was going to regret this, but she owed him, far more than she could ever repay him.

But this would be a start.

"I can speak the demonic tongue, ancient fae, and modern fae, and even some of the lesser known languages of Hell."

He frowned over his shoulder at her and bit out, "Good for you."

Meow.

This kitty had claws when he thought he was being rubbed the wrong way.

She wasn't looking for a fight with him though.

"I'm saying I can help you."

He stopped so suddenly she almost slammed into his back and instinctively pushed her hands out in front of her.

Planting them right on his bare hips.

Stupid backpack. Her face heated. If he hadn't been wearing it, she probably would have aimed her hands at his back and not somewhere lower, and more dangerous.

Damn. His muscles were as firm as they looked beneath her palms.

His head bent, the wilder lengths of his short silver hair falling forwards as he looked down.

At her hands.

Lyra snatched them back.

"Why would you help me?"

The way he said that, filled with incredulity and confusion, had her heart softening again, and wanting to know more about him. Why did he find it so impossible that she might want to help him?

Why was he looking for a new place to call home?

What had driven him away from his pride?

"Because you helped me." She kept her eyes locked on the back of his head, and her feelings steady, crushing the part of her that said she couldn't trust him. She couldn't trust any male.

She didn't have to trust him in order to help him.

Once they were square, she would leave as planned, would head right through that portal and not look back.

"Fine," he said, and he could have sounded more appreciative of her help. She glared at the back of his head. He started walking again.

"We can start at the village. It's the first location in the document I have."

She wasn't familiar with the village in question. She followed Grey down the rest of the way to the valley floor, mulling over everything he had told her. She was no longer sure that getting a clearer picture of him had been a good idea.

It painted him in too good a light.

It made it harder for her to keep her distance.

"We can rest here." He jerked his chin towards a few black rocks that had obviously tumbled down the mountain at some point.

Lyra eased her bottom down against one of them and bit back a sigh as she lifted the weight from her legs. The bone in her left one had fully healed, but it was still sore and it ached from all the walking. She wouldn't tell Grey that though. He would probably offer to carry her or something equally as noble and kind.

She wasn't sure she could take it.

He pulled a cloth from his back pocket, huffed and sank down onto a boulder opposite her, resting there as he rubbed the cloth across his face and neck.

Gods.

She shouldn't have looked at him.

Sweat glistened on his bare skin, tempting her eyes to go to places they shouldn't, to traverse muscles that screamed of strength that called to her on a deep level, one where she wasn't quite master. They tugged at every instinct, filling her head with images she shouldn't be entertaining, but couldn't quite block out.

He paused at his work and looked across at her, those soft blue eyes turning hard and dark with something that stoked the fire inside her, pulled harder at her and lured her towards him.

She was about to force herself to look away when he closed his eyes and frowned, lowered his head and fisted his hands in his lap.

What was he struggling against whenever he did that?

She feared the answer, even as part of her ached to know it.

When he finally opened his eyes again, they were calm and cool, the fire of passion gone from them.

He pushed onto his feet, jammed the cloth into his back pocket and turned side on to her, his eyes locking on the distance.

"We should keep moving." He didn't sound as if he wanted to do that. His deep voice was thick and hoarse, a low murmur that sent a tremor through her, a rolling wave that brought heat in its wake.

She forced herself to nod and eased back onto her feet.

Grey glanced down at them and looked as if he wanted to apologise again. He had offered his boots to her, but she had refused. They would be too big for her and she was used to walking barefoot now.

His socks were a blessing though.

They cushioned her feet enough that she didn't feel the sharp bite of the rough ground as they began walking again, heading across the valley basin towards the village in the distance. She could just about make out the glow of flaming torches, a tiny flicker of gold in the dim light.

Returning to the mortal world, to her home, was going to feel like Heaven after being surrounded by so much gloominess for the past few months.

He adjusted his pace to match hers so they were walking side by side across the black land.

He was too quiet again, trapped by thoughts that she wanted to know, not because she wanted to pry into his private life but because she hated the dreadful silence and the rattling of her chains.

"We can find someone to break them," he said, and she felt sure he had read her mind until she realised she was toying with the chains, had been tugging at them without realising it. "I need to get them off you."

I need.

Not *we* need.

Most people would have spoken of them as a group, with a shared desire.

Grey had spoken only of himself, of a need that he had, one that looked as if it was eating away at him judging by the way he was glaring at the handcuffs, a flare of anger in his eyes.

He reached for them and she hissed at him, a reaction she couldn't quite contain. His hand stilled, and he stood frozen for a moment and then backed off.

"Sorry." She rubbed at the cuffs, shame sweeping through her.

He had only wanted to look at them, but she hadn't been able to stop herself from lashing out at him, driven by the sudden fear that had gripped her.

Fear that something bad would happen to her as it had every time someone had touched her shackles.

He shook his head, his blue eyes flooding with a soft look. "I should be the one apologising."

She closed her hand around her right cuff and held it near her chest as she battled for the words she wanted to say, the ones to reassure him that he had no reason to apologise to her. She had been the one to automatically assume he was going to hurt her. She was the one in the wrong.

"No, Grey. I… it's just… whenever someone touched them…" Her voice grew tight and a weight pressed down on her chest.

She wasn't strong enough to talk about it yet after all.

Grey gently shook his head again. "I won't do it again. I didn't mean to drag anything up. I was just going to see if I could break the chains off them."

She looked down at her cuffs. "I managed to snap the chain in half, but the links nearer to the rings on them are stronger."

Meaning he wouldn't be able to break them.

He wasn't like her. He was a feline shifter, and was powerful, but hellcats were the strongest of their kind. If she couldn't break them, then he certainly wouldn't be able to do it. Even with the shackles sucking on her strength, she was stronger than him.

"I'd like to try," he said in a low voice, one laced with determination, and a promise that he wouldn't hurt her.

He wasn't going to let it go unless she gave him a shot at them. She could see it in his eyes, in the way he couldn't take them off the chains. It tore her in two, ripped her between letting him try and fail to alleviate his need, and pushing him away to protect herself.

She wanted them gone too.

She tugged at them, weighing her options. If she gave him a shot at them, it might stop him from looking at them and reminding her that they were there.

She drew down a deep breath and followed it with another, trying to find some balance and courage, something she had always had before that cursed male had tricked her and sold her into slavery.

She could do this.

Grey would fail, and he would let it go.

When she returned home, she would find all the saws and tools she owned and get the damned things off her.

She released the death grip she had on her right shackle and held it out to him, her arm shaking as she edged it towards him. Her heart began a sickening fast rhythm against her chest.

His eyes leaped between the cuff and her. "You're sure."

She nodded, swallowed to wet her dry throat, and sucked down another breath. "Just… don't touch my skin."

Because she wasn't sure she could take it and she feared what might happen. Her animal side was pushing, fear pulling it to the fore because it was her stronger form, one she could use to fight and would ensure her victory.

Grey wasn't going to hurt her. She didn't need to fight him.

He was going to make a few attempts on the chain and then he would give up.

"Close your eyes," he whispered.

She did as he had instructed, shutting out the delicious sight of him and focusing on picturing her home in Norway, deep in the mountains, miles away from the humans and the busy mortal world.

That vision flickered and faded as she felt him take hold of the shackle, but she clawed it back again, breathed through the sudden rush of panic and managed to keep her feet planted to the black dirt. She could do this.

Grey wasn't going to hurt her.

He drew down a deep breath.

He would make a few attempts on the chain.

He roared.

Her arm jerked to her left.

Chain hit rock with a startling clamour.

Her eyes flicked open.

She stared in disbelief at her right cuff, at the empty half-ring where the chain had been attached to it, and then at Grey.

He stood before her, chest straining, shoulders tensed and eyes dark.

Either she had been wrong about how strong she was with the cuffs inhibiting her, or Grey was far more powerful than she had imagined.

Far more powerful than he should have been.

"What species are you?" she whispered, afraid of his answer.

He wasn't a hellcat.

But her heart leaped around in her chest as if he might be, her breath stuttering and refusing to come.

He took hold of her other cuff in one hand and the chain attached to it in his other.

"Tiger."

He roared again as he pulled on the chain and shoved at the cuff, moving them in opposite directions. His fangs lengthened, his dark silver eyebrows meeting hard above his closed eyes, and every muscle on his chest and arms tensed in unison.

Lyra could only stare at him as he snapped the chain on her cuffs. It took effort, strength that left him visibly shaking as he tossed the chain away from them, but he managed it.

She had never met a tiger shifter before. Were they all as strong as Grey?

He stooped, picked up the other chain, and growled as he twisted away from her and threw it far into the distance.

Grey shifted to face her, looked down at her wrists, and exhaled hard. "That's better."

He was telling her.

Lyra looked down at her cuffs.

Damn, it felt good to see the chains gone.

She only wished she could find a way to get out of the shackles too. All in good time, she supposed. She would get them off her.

"Come on," Grey said and tilted his head towards the village. "First round is on me as a thank you for letting me do that."

She should be the one thanking him again. She stared at the metal bands around her wrists as she walked, following him to the huts and tents in the distance. If she had coin, or anything of worth, she would buy him as many rounds as he wanted.

"I think I should probably translate for you before we start drinking," she said and he smiled over his shoulder at her. "Do they have food too?"

"Not sure… but if you like protein bars, I have plenty." His smile widened and a light filled his eyes, one that warmed her.

He was relieved, happy that the chains were gone.

Just how big was that heart he was protecting?

She wanted to know.

She shook that away and focused on her plan, the one where she was meant to thank him for rescuing her by helping him talk with the locals and then leaving once he knew where he was meant to go next.

As they neared the boundary wall of the village, she lifted her head and looked around. A few ramshackle black huts stood in the centre of the low stone ring, with tents erected nearer to the wall. People of all different species moved around the village, some in groups of two or three, at least thirty in total. It was busy.

She had pictured it as a quiet group of thatched stone huts where people lived, but it looked more like a way station.

She limped forwards, and a few of the females and males coming and going looked her way.

An urge to fight swept through her and she struggled to control it, to bring it to heel and overcome it.

It was instinct, that was all. She was injured, felt weak and vulnerable, and so her instincts were making her react and want to lash out to protect herself.

"You'll be fine," Grey murmured quietly next to her, and she realised he had dropped back and had moved closer to her.

Had he sensed she was on edge?

"I won't let anything happen to you."

Lyra looked up at his profile. His dark silver eyebrows were low above those mesmerising blue eyes of his, which were dark as he studied the people moving around the village, focusing on those closest to her.

She looked at them too. They weren't a threat to her. She had no need to fight them. Her eyes roamed back to Grey. Calm washed through her, pushing out the urge to bloody her claws.

He led her into the largest of the circular black stone huts. It was busy.

The urge to fight returned as people looked at Grey, and then at her. She bit back a growl as Grey ushered her through the cramped room towards the small bar, pushing his way through the crowd. She used him as a blocker, staying close to him so no one would brush against her. When they reached the stone bar, he offered her the only seat, and used his body as a shield, keeping her safe as he had promised.

That calm returned.

It dissipated the moment he hailed the bartender, a curvy brunette with a killer smile, enough cleavage to drown a man stuffed into a tiny leather corset, and dazzling colourful eyes made for luring males to their doom.

The second the female looked his way, Lyra saw red and the urge to fight flooded her, had her black claws extending and a snarl curling up her throat.

That left her cold.

The need to fight wasn't hitting her whenever someone looked at her, born of a need to protect herself because she was injured.

It was striking her whenever he looked at a female.

Lyra gripped her knees as that hit her, stared at the black stone bar in front of her and struggled to find a valid reason for her reaction, one other than the obvious.

These females weren't hellcats. She had no reason to want to fight them for territory, an instinct that ruled all female hellcats and was why she had avoided Hell and her own kind for most of her five hundred years.

Yet she couldn't stop herself. She wanted to hurt them.

Kill them.

She tried to shake it off, fear rising inside her.

The female reached them and Lyra focused on her work, trying to shut out that dark need to fight that pushed her to lash out at the woman.

"I need information about a group of mortal hunters seen around this part of Hell," Grey said.

Lyra translated it into the ancient fae tongue.

The female looked Grey over, stoking Lyra's urge to fight the bitch, and then looked off to her left, towards a shadowy corner away from the bar.

"Speak with him." The bartender pointed at a lone male seated at one of the tables.

Grey looked at Lyra.

"There's a male who might be able to help us." She slipped from the stool when Grey moved off, and managed to smile at the bartender as she said, "Thanks."

Grey prowled through the busy room and she followed on his heels, flashing fangs at a few of the females who looked their way.

"You know of mortals in these parts?" Grey said, voice darker than before, and she wondered what had gotten into him.

She stepped around him.

Oh my.

The male the bartender had told her to speak with lounged in a wooden chair made for two, arms stretched along the back and his right ankle casually resting on his left knee. Black trousers hugged his long legs, polished leather riding boots reaching his knees, and a matching black tunic fitted snug to his lean figure.

Violet eyes lifted to her and the tips of his ears grew a little more pointed, poking out of his wavy blue-black hair.

An elf.

"I don't speak his language," she said to Grey, but he wasn't listening.

He was glaring at the male.

"I do speak yours," the elf offered and swept his right hand out towards the space beside him. "Come. Let us speak of mortals."

Grey pushed past her and sat where the elf had wanted her to be, his broad frame shoving the male to one side, pinning him into the corner of the chair.

"Speak then, Elf." He pulled a stack of folded papers out of his backpack and slammed them down on the table. "I need to know where this place is they speak of here."

"Why not just skip straight to this entry?" The male pressed a finger to the paper further down the page. "I can tell you where this place is."

Grey looked closely at the papers, some of the darkness leaving his eyes as he read whatever was on them at the point the elf had marked. She tried to see, but it was impossible to read when it was upside down to her.

She moved to her right, coming around the table.

Grey lifted his head and a strange sensation built inside her as he stared at her.

She stopped moving towards the elf to get a better angle on the papers and looked at Grey.

Right into eyes that were bright blue in the low light, glowing around his pupils.

An unsettling feeling went through her.

One that whispered Grey was experiencing the same dark need that kept trying to consume her.

The urge to fight.

CHAPTER 7

The ferocity of the feeling that swept through Grey the moment the elf looked at Lyra shook him to his core.

It was strong, overpowering, commanding him to fight.

For her.

He tried to focus on the elf and on finding out what the male knew, but it became impossible when Lyra moved closer to the male.

Grey's hands shook as his claws lengthened.

His fangs emerged, itching for the taste of blood.

His heart slammed against his chest.

He grabbed the papers and his bag. "Excuse me a moment."

He was out of the door before Lyra could say anything, had placed at least thirty metres between him and the village in the next heartbeat.

Leaving her with the male.

Grey growled, his fangs punching long from his gums and his claws sinking into the straps of the backpack as he slung it over his shoulders.

The hunger to shift and rip out the elf's throat blasted through him.

He forced himself to keep moving away, to place more distance between them and find some space, some air, anything to help him get the urges running rampant through him back under control.

He was halfway across the valley before it finally began to abate and he could breathe again.

"Wait."

Lyra.

He made the mistake of turning towards her.

The second he saw her, a different urge struck him, this one far more powerful than the need to fight.

He needed to dominate her and drive her into submission. It wasn't him, and he didn't like how it made him feel. He didn't like it at all. He wasn't one to force his will on anyone.

He was a protector first and foremost, a male who took care of others not one who did things that would hurt them.

He breathed hard, desperately trying to subdue the instincts rising inside him before she reached him and saw what she did to him, and the things he wanted to do with her.

He couldn't let her see it. She was terrified of males now, afraid of anyone touching her. He didn't want to frighten her. It would kill him as sure as a blade through his heart.

"Wait." She held her hand up as she limped towards him, a wild edge to her blue eyes, one that had him waiting for her when he should have kept walking and putting more distance between them.

With her injury slowing her down, he could easily outrun her and leave her in the dust, unable to follow him.

It was pointless.

He could outrun her, but he couldn't outrun this feeling, the urges that struck him and tried to control him whenever he let himself slip.

They were never going away.

He stared at Lyra.

Because she was his fated one.

That killed him.

He couldn't take it.

"The elf says it's in the dragon realm." She stopped near him and leaned forwards as she fought to catch her breath. "You left before he could say. Why?"

She lifted her chin and hit him hard with those blue eyes, her black hair falling forwards to brush both of her cheeks.

"Thanks." Grey turned away from her because he couldn't bear looking at her, wasn't sure he was strong enough right now, not in the wake of the revelation that she was his fated female.

He had thought he would never have one, yet here she was, the one who had been made for him and him alone.

A female for him to cherish, to protect and to love forever.

But she would never be that for him. He wasn't a fool. He could see the damage her captivity had done to her, how it had shaped her feelings about males and about anything that might be a collar, whether it was a physical restraint, or a blood bond.

She would hate it, and hate him for it.

He started walking again, his heart leaping about all over the place in his chest, a need to turn back around and stay with her warring with a deeper need to leave.

He didn't want to hurt her.

He might if he stayed near her.

He wouldn't be able to live with himself if he lost control and did something he would regret.

Something she would regret too when she realised what he was.

He didn't think he could bear her inevitable rejection.

"Thanks?" she snapped, a sharp edge to her usually soft voice. "*Thanks?* That's all you have to say to me?"

"You helped me. We're even. Just keep on the same bearing we took to reach the village and you'll hit the portal. Go home, Lyra." Gods, those were the hardest words he had ever had to say.

She didn't want to be around him though, and she had done what she had promised. She had translated for him and now he had a lead to follow. She was free to go. He had things from here.

After everything she had been through in Hell, she was probably already walking away from him, taking him up on the offer.

Only when he focused on her, he found she was moving closer instead of further away.

He looked over his shoulder at her. "What are you doing?"

"My debt is far from repaid, and I know the way to the dragon realm." She scowled at him. "I'm going to help you."

Gods.

He couldn't bear it.

The need to crush her in his arms, to bruise her lips with a fierce kiss that would make her see that she was his, and his alone, and he was hers, was too strong, consuming, driving him to do something. He couldn't do this. He couldn't take her with him.

He wasn't strong enough to keep fighting that need.

She was asking too much of him.

"Just point the way," he bit out. "You're not coming with me. I don't need your help anymore."

"You do." Stubborn hellcat. She planted her hands on her hips. "It's better this way."

No. It was better his way. It was better for both of them.

"Go." He reached out to grab her and push her away from him.

She bared her fangs at him and hissed.

His hand dropped to his side, self-loathing sweeping through him. He had almost overstepped the line already. If they stayed together, he would end up doing something terrible. He would cross that line in the worst of ways.

It wasn't him.

But at the same time it was.

He had never been aware of his hellcat side, but now he was aware of nothing else. It ruled him, pushed him into seizing Lyra with both hands and bending her to his will, doing whatever it took to make her belong to him.

No.

He closed his eyes, clenched his fists and swore he would never be that male.

Because Lyra was leaving him right here, right now, and he would never see her again.

She started walking, moving away from him, and relief poured through him, lifting some of the weight from his heart. Thank the gods, she was going to do as he asked and leave him.

It was what he deserved.

He didn't belong with a female like her.

He didn't deserve any female.

Even if he had managed to control his dark urges around her, eventually she would have seen him shift, and she would have witnessed him in his feline form.

She would have seen him as his pride did.

Not a beautiful tiger with gold and black fur like his twin and the rest of his family.

An aberration.

A freak.

The relief that had washed through him like cool water dried up when he focused harder on Lyra.

And realised she was heading in the opposite direction to the portal, walking towards the mountains they had traversed to reach the valley from the one on the other side where the slave camp had been.

He opened his eyes and looked at her as she limped determinedly away from him, his black t-shirt and cargo shorts swamping her slender figure, and her skin marred with dark dust that reached halfway up her calves.

"Where are you going?"

She didn't look at him as she answered.

"I just remembered I had some business in the dragon realm."

CHAPTER 8

Something was eating away at Grey again. Lyra had thought him distant and quiet before, but since the village he had shown her that it had been the mere tip of a very cold, very forbidding iceberg.

He had barely said a word to her in the past day.

The few times he had spoken, most of them had been attempts to make her leave him.

Why?

She had said she would translate for him, and she would.

Although part of her still wasn't sure why she hadn't taken the out he had given to her.

With everything she had been through at the hands of males, when he had offered her directions to the nearest portal and told her to leave, she had expected to take him up on it.

Something had made her stay.

She wanted to say it was that feeling that he was far from home. Alone in this dark realm.

Lonely.

It still struck that chord in her, even more so as she walked beside him. There was only ten foot of space between them, but it felt like an ocean. She felt alone, even when she wasn't. Lonely.

It was Grey.

He was too quiet, hadn't spoken to her in over three hours now. That time he had wanted her to leave, but something in his eyes had said he didn't mean it, so rather than arguing, she had just kept walking.

How long had it been since he had last asked how her leg was doing and whether she needed a rest?

She was starting to miss that gentle, caring side of him. The cold front had closed in shortly afterwards, chilling the air between them, that much she did recall.

Okay, so maybe that was partly her fault since she hadn't been able to hold back the urge to bare her fangs at him, the thought that he believed her weak and vulnerable still pushing her to threaten him.

He wasn't a threat to her though.

She knew that deep in her heart.

He had merely been concerned about her, hadn't viewed her injury as a weakness he could exploit to overpower her or hurt her.

She had no reason not to trust him after everything he had done for her, yet she couldn't bring herself to have faith in him. Had she lost her ability to trust? Was she always going to feel this way, act this way?

Had she closed herself off?

Her gaze slid towards Grey. She wanted to trust him.

Fuck, she wanted more than just trust between them.

It had been slowly dawning on her from the moment she had first seen him, and now she couldn't shake it. The need to fight the females who looked at him in the village had been the last clue, the one that had helped her see the truth.

She wanted him.

Desired him.

He was gorgeous, a warrior with a big heart, an enticing blend of dangerous and tender that drew her to him, made her ache with a need to know more about him and move closer still, until she was under his skin as deeply as he was under hers.

"Do you need a break? Are you hungry?"

Gods, she had missed the sound of his voice. It hit her hard, left her feeling she had gone days, weeks without hearing it rather than a handful of hours. She soaked it in, savoured it as she would water in the driest desert.

He only ever seemed concerned about her. She couldn't remember ever meeting someone like that—someone like him.

Was he ever concerned about himself?

Would he just keep walking, not resting nor eating, unless she said she wanted it?

"I still can't believe you charged into a slave auction to free everyone." She let the words slip from her lips, a gentle outpouring of her feelings that she hoped might entice him into talking to her, telling her more about himself.

So she could learn to trust him.

"I couldn't stop myself," he said and then sighed, his bare chest expanding with it.

She resisted the urge to look at it and kept her eyes locked on his profile. "At first, I thought you might be someone from the auction."

He stopped and when she looked back at him, he was scowling at her, his eyes dark and silvery brows knitted hard above them.

"I know better now. You can't blame me for not trusting you." She hoped he didn't anyway. She hadn't really thought about how he might take it. The words had just come out. Maybe she wanted to open up a little to him too, to allow him to get to know her better. "You have to admit, most people would have watched that procession march past and then carried on with their lives."

"It was just something I had to do." He shrugged and started walking again, long legs carrying him back towards her and then past her.

She followed him over a small hill and down the other side, towards the base of a mountain that cut a valley in half down the centre. "Because of what happened to your sister and your brother? You must have been raised well."

He rolled his shoulders again and she had the feeling he didn't want to talk about it.

Surprise swept through her when he spoke.

"Maybe. My position in the pride was that of protector." He adjusted the left strap of his backpack, far too interested in it.

Avoiding her.

Why?

A lot of things she had been admiring about him suddenly made a lot of sense, and no matter what angle she looked at it from, it didn't paint him in a bad light at all.

"What did you protect?" Curiosity firmly took hold of the helm and steered her towards getting an answer to that question.

When she had first met him, she had formed an instant opinion of him—he was a warrior, a male born for war and honed by it, one who obeyed the call of violence.

She couldn't have been more wrong.

The warrior was still there when she looked at him, but he had proven himself so much more than that.

He looked at her out of the corner of his eye again, sighed and fixed his gaze ahead of them. "My little sister."

The one who had found her mate.

She wanted to smile at that, at the thought of him playing the role of bodyguard to his sister. Beneath the growly exterior was a big heart that beat with a need to protect the innocent.

He had said he had attacked the auction because of what had happened to his sister and brother, but it was more than that, she felt sure of it. He would have done the same thing even if his sister and brother hadn't been held captive in the past.

It was just the male he was.

His need to protect would have driven him to serve justice the slavers and free everyone.

"So do you protect the pride now that your sister is mated?"

He didn't look at her. "No."

And that sensation she had about him, that loneliness she picked up in him, made sense at last.

His role in life, the mission that had probably been his and his alone to fulfil for decades or more, had suddenly come to an end and he had been replaced by another male, the role of protecting his sister passed on to her mate.

Had there been nothing to keep him at the pride?

Hellcats were solitary, but as far as she knew, tigers weren't. They were a pride animal, one who thrived while surrounded by others of their kind. What had driven him to turn his back on them and walk away?

It was more than just this mission for his brother.

Something had made him leave.

Something she wanted to know.

She stared at his profile, struggling with the urge to ask, afraid of taking that step closer to him. How was it possible to want something and not want it at the same time?

To want someone but not want them?

Was it just fear of getting hurt again that had her taking a step away whenever she really wanted to move one closer? She was afraid to trust again after what had happened to her.

She studied Grey's handsome face and those eyes that told her everything he was feeling even when he wanted to hide it from her. Now that she was starting to know him better, she could see she had been wrong about him. He wasn't good at hiding his feelings at all.

They were always there in his eyes even if his face remained impassive, unreadable.

Those eyes told her everything.

They slid towards her, softened and gained a warmth that reached out to her and offered comfort. They stirred a feeling in her, one even her battered and bruised heart couldn't deny.

If anyone could give her a reason to trust again, it was Grey.

She lost herself in his eyes, in that silent promise they made, the one that said he would never hurt her, not if he could help it.

He would protect her.

His lips moved, and she struggled to focus on them, to tear her thoughts away from how beautiful his eyes were as they swore that to her.

His words registered one by one.

"Enough about me. I want to know how a hellcat ends up living in Norway."

She stared at his mouth, her own turning dry as she thought about what he was really proposing.

He wanted to know more than just the story of how a creature born of fire and brimstone ended up living in the frozen north of Europe.

He wanted to break down the barrier between them and move closer to her.

Lyra swallowed her fear.

She could do this.

Because she wanted to move closer to him too.

CHAPTER 9

Grey found it impossible to keep his eyes off Lyra as she walked beside him, her limp less pronounced now. She didn't help when she took to twirling a length of her long black hair around the fingers of her left hand, pulling his focus there.

To those nails made for raking down his back.

The urge to dominate her rose back to the fore and pushed him to obey it, to turn and take that delicate hand of hers and force it against his chest and make her touch him, stroke him as she was stroking her hair.

He gritted his teeth and shoved back against it, refusing to succumb to it.

The gods only knew how, but he drove it back into submission enough that he could concentrate on Lyra and learning more about her.

He wasn't sure why he needed to know.

It had been a gut reaction to her asking questions about his life, and about him.

Learning more about her was likely to be a mistake.

When she finally left him, walked out of his life and never looked back, she would haunt him now, everything he knew about her bringing her to life in his mind and making it difficult to forget about her.

To go on without her.

His claws extended, his heart provoking them into emerging as it whispered to him, told him to seize hold of her and not let her leave him. She had been made for him, and he needed to show her that she belonged to him now.

He needed to claim her.

No.

He curled his hands into fists and grimaced as his claws bit into his palms, and he caught the tinny scent of his own blood in the air. He focused on the pain, imagined it to be a thousand times worse, cutting at his heart, shredding his soul. That pain was what he would inflict on Lyra if he allowed the dark urges that gripped him to get the better of him.

He would be no better than the people who had held her captive, or the sick bastard who might own her now if he hadn't intervened in the auction.

"Grey?" Lyra's soft voice chased away his black thoughts, shining through the clouds that marred his mind again, bringing light back into his soul. "What's wrong?"

He realised he had stopped walking and was stood in the middle of the valley as still as a statue and staring at her.

Scaring her.

He shook his head. "Nothing."

She lowered her blue gaze, and pointed. "Your hands."

Grey looked down at them. Blood dripped from between his clenched fingers.

He pulled the cloth from the back pocket of his black fatigues, turned his back on her and wiped the blood away. More pooled in the deep cuts his claws had made.

Lyra took a step towards him.

"It's nothing," he bit out, a little harshly judging by how she backed off. "I was just… I'm fine now."

He wasn't.

He was far from fine.

The thought of a male owning Lyra still had his blood running hot, a need to hunt and kill colliding with a terrible need to stake a claim on her.

He drew down a deep breath and held it in his lungs, but he couldn't centre himself, couldn't find the peace he normally found whenever he used this calming technique.

His blood still raged.

"I just need a minute," he whispered, hating the sound of his voice as he admitted that.

He sounded weak.

Would Lyra think him weak now?

A male easily overcome by his emotions?

He sucked down another breath, and exhaled it slowly, emptying his lungs. This time it worked, pushed all the fury out of his blood and let cool calm rush in to fill him.

He didn't look at Lyra as he turned back around and started walking again.

She was silent as she hurried to catch up with him, and as she fell into step beside him, and even as they crossed the end of the mountain that jutted out into the valley, cutting it in two.

"I don't really like Hell," she whispered, as if she was afraid to speak to him now, feared that she might reawaken the darkness that had gripped him, but then her voice gained strength, confidence that eased his heart and lightened it, lifting some of the load from it as they walked. "It's horrible, isn't it?"

He silently thanked her for it, for the fact she cared about him enough to want to make him feel better and wanted to be around him still when he had proven himself unpredictable and had shown her that he wasn't fully in control of himself.

Gods, he should have fought better to hide it from her.

He didn't want her to feel she couldn't trust him, or believe him liable to hurt her at any moment.

"I prefer things back home," she said, her voice light and bright.

When he risked a glance at her, she was smiling, her blue eyes shining with it, as if just thinking about home was enough to chase all her troubles away.

He wished it was the same for him.

Thinking about home left him hollow inside.

What was it like to have a home that made you feel that way?

"Let me see." She pursed her lips, and he mentally cursed when he realised he had asked that out loud, revealing yet another part of himself to her that he had wanted to keep hidden.

He didn't want her to think he was lost, even when he was.

She smiled a little wider, but he could see through it, could see the thoughts crossing her mind as she looked at him. She wanted to know why he didn't feel the pride was his home.

He couldn't tell her.

He didn't want her to know that much about him.

She would end up looking at him the same way his pride did.

He could bear it from them, was used to it now having been subjected to it since birth.

But the thought of Lyra looking at him with contempt, with disgust.

It would destroy him.

"I think I like the quiet. The solitude and the freedom. It's just me now. My mother and aunt passed on decades ago, but they taught me well, and my mother loved me deeply even though my father was a monster who held her and my aunt as slaves—"

"Gods, Lyra." Grey couldn't hold back those words as hers hit him. He stopped and stared at her, reeling from what she had told him.

Her mother had been a slave.

Lyra scoffed. "I'm sure the bastard got what he deserved. That's the trouble with hellcat males. They always think they can just take what they want… that we females belong to them and should just hurl ourselves at their feet and be their breeding bitches and not complain about it."

Those words hit him harder and he almost staggered back a step as the force of her anger and her hatred hit him with each one, hammered into him and pierced his soul.

She despised male hellcats.

She feared what they did to the females of her kind.

Things he wanted to do to her.

He closed his eyes, unable to bring himself to look at her when there was so much fury and fear in her eyes, feelings she would have towards him if she knew the truth about him.

He would deserve her wrath too, would deserve her giving him hell and walking right out of his life.

He wouldn't blame her for it.

"I should have known better than to trust one of them."

For a dreadful heartbeat of time, he thought she knew about his ancestry and was talking about him.

"Gods, I was an idiot. He said he would help me track down more females from my family… I knew I shouldn't have trusted him."

Grey slowly opened his eyes and lifted them, running them over her baggy shorts and t-shirt to her face. Her eyes glowed blue, the fires of her breed burning in them, and fangs flashed between her lips as she spat the words.

"The bastard collared me and sold me."

He growled low in his throat, his own fangs emerging as her words hit him, conjuring an image of her shackled by someone she had trusted.

Betrayed.

The urge to shift swept through him and he breathed hard against it, fear of her seeing him for what he was holding it back. It grew stronger as he looked at her, and the need to hunt and kill, to bloody claw and fang for her sake blasted through him and drove him to obey it.

"Grey," she whispered, no fear in her voice, only a strange sense of awe, as if she was touched by how he had reacted, not terrified.

She stared into his eyes, and he grew aware of them, of the fact that his were probably glowing, and would be in danger of revealing his heritage to her if they hadn't already been blue because of his defective genes.

"Is he the reason you're so far from home?" It was hard to keep his voice measured and even when he wanted to roar, wanted to bellow his rage so everyone in Hell would hear it.

Including the male she had been tricked into trusting.

A hellcat.

Like him.

Gods, she would never trust him if she knew the truth about him.

He could see that now.

He had thought it before, but even as he had thought it, he had been fooling himself into not believing it, into holding on to the sliver of hope that she might find it in her heart to love him.

It broke through the illusion he had constructed in his heart and hit home with a force that shook him.

No matter what he did, no matter how fiercely he fought his urges and kept them in check for her, she would never feel anything for him.

She would never be his.

He wasn't sure when he had started wanting her to be that for him, needing her to be his mate and his forever, but it was over now.

"I don't want to talk about him…" She looked away, turning her profile to him, and sighed. "I was stupid and made a mistake, but it's over now, and I'm free… thanks to you."

Would she still be thanking him if she knew what he was?

Would she trust him?

"We should keep moving. Hell has a way of sneaking up on you if you stay in one place too long." She took a few steps and looked back at him when he didn't move. "Are you coming?"

Her hand twitched at her side, as if she wanted to hold it out to him and coax him towards her.

Hell, he wished that she would, that she would reach for him in the way he kept wanting to reach for her, to pull her closer to him.

He forced himself to nod and started after her when she began walking again. When she tried moving closer to him, he drifted away, keeping at least fifteen feet between them, a distance that seemed to work for him and eased the need to gather her into his arms and kiss her until she surrendered to him.

Gods, he bet her lips were as soft as they looked.

He had kissed a female once, a mortal. It had been strange, unsettling, but once he had overcome his nerves, had convinced himself that she would have no reason to despise him because she didn't know his kind existed, it had been nice.

"What did you mean when you said Hell has a way of sneaking up on you?" He kept his eyes away from her as he tried to push aside thoughts of kissing her.

It wasn't going to happen.

Unlike the mortal, she was aware of his kind and his breed, and she wouldn't sully herself with him like that. Not if she knew the truth about him.

"There are beasts in this realm that like eating stray cats. It's better we avoid attracting their attention by remaining in the open for too long." Her blue eyes roamed the mountain to their left and the valley ahead of them.

"You know a lot about Hell for someone who doesn't live here. Did you live here once?"

She shook her head, gathered her hair in both hands and lifted it away from her neck. Damp strands stuck to her skin, drawing his eyes downwards.

To her nape.

A lightning bolt struck hard inside him, from his fangs down to his balls, and he grimaced as his entire body tightened in response, muscles clamping down hard on his bones.

The need to sink his fangs into that sweet nape, to claim her as his own, broke over him and he barely bit back the growl that rolled up his throat in response.

Lyra slowly lowered her hair as if she was aware of his eyes on her and the need that surged through him.

"Look at it. Who would want to live here?" She sounded casual, but he could sense her nerves, how he had unsettled her by staring at that spot on her neck where he would need to bite in order to place a claim on her.

He forced himself to take his eyes off her and take in his surroundings.

Black mountains rose ahead of them in a long range that stretched so far in both directions that it blended into the darkness. The golden glow from beyond them silhouetted their jagged peaks. They were forbidding, as grim as the rest of Hell, and the closer he got to the Devil's lands, the hotter the air became. It was stuffy, had sweat sliding down his spine beneath his backpack.

"It isn't a patch on the human world." It wasn't hard to admit that.

Fresh air, clean water, and lush nature versus humid, liable to poison you and grim black?

Hardly a competition.

"It's not just their world." Lyra frowned over her shoulder at him. "It's your world as much as it is theirs. For as long as mortals have lived in it, shifters have too. Hell, dragons were king there once."

"That was a long time ago." Way beyond his years and any lifespan of a feline shifter. "Before someone stripped them of their throne and plunged them into Hell."

It was a story that had fascinated him as a cub, one his mother had often told him as a cautionary tale when it was time for his nap. The dragons had grown too big for their boots and someone had dealt with them.

When he had grown older, he had read all he could about it, which wasn't much. No one seemed to know the real reason the dragons had been banished and cursed to live out their lives in Hell.

His urges finally began to level out, falling back to a manageable level, and he breathed easily again, able to enjoy Lyra's company once more without fearing he might hurt her or drive her away.

She froze.

Her eyes locked ahead of her.

The instinct to fight and protect her had him instantly whirling on the spot, scouring the bleak lands for whatever she had spotted that had spooked her.

In the distance, he could make out something. He squinted and focused. Bodies. Two of them.

The scent of blood hit him.

Old. Decaying.

Lyra took off towards them, running at full speed.

"Lyra, no."

She wasn't listening. She raced towards the bodies, her heartbeat off the scale, her fear flooding his own veins.

He growled and gave chase, his backpack bouncing against his bare back with each long stride.

The second he was close enough, he reached out and grabbed her wrist.

She snarled, turned on him and smacked his hand away, sending pain shooting up his bones. The moment she realised what she had done, her hand fell to her side and she looked down at her feet.

"Sorry. I didn't mean it." Her voice was a broken whisper, one that tore at him together with the feelings he could detect in her—the pain and the fear, and the regret.

Grey withdrew a step to give her more space. "I know. It's instinctive. You're afraid of me."

And it hurt like hell.

He didn't want her to fear him, didn't want her lashing out at him whenever he dared to touch her. It cut at him, carving a hole in his heart.

She shook her head, her black hair brushing her shoulders. "I'm not… I just…"

He walked past her and crouched beside the bodies, giving her a moment to pull herself back together. Giving himself a moment too, because he needed one, needed to get hold of his feelings again and clamp down on them.

It was a fucking mess.

Not his emotions, but the two corpses in front of him.

Something had ripped the females to shreds.

He eyed the shackles on their wrists. Whoever they had been, they had escaped when he had attacked the slave camp.

And they had met a grisly end.

"What did this?" Grey looked up at Lyra as she came to a halt beside him. "Those creatures you were talking about?"

She stared at the corpses, her face paling. The fear he had felt in her grew stronger. It shone in her blue eyes as she slowly lifted her hands and twisted them together in front of her breasts, rubbing at her shackles.

A chill went through him.

It hadn't been a something that had ripped the poor females to pieces with its claws.

It had been a someone.

"*Who* did this, Lyra?" He rose to his feet and stepped between her and the corpses, so she was staring at his chest instead. "I'm getting the feeling you know… and I want to know what we're up against."

Her eyes leaped up to his, shock flaring in them and her feelings.

Because he had said '*we're*', treating them as partners. He wanted to be more than that with her, even when he knew it was impossible.

"I can't protect you unless I know what I'm up against." And he would protect her, even if whatever had killed the females ended up killing him too.

He would give his life for her.

She looked back down at his chest, stared straight through it as if she could still see the corpses. "I can't be certain, but I saw him once, during an inspection close to the dragon realm… a few weeks after they had captured me."

"Who?"

Her blue eyes lifted to meet his again. "A fallen angel."

Shit. That wasn't good.

"He ripped one of the slavers apart because he had failed to inform him straight away that he had procured a hellcat."

He liked the sound of that even less. It had a cold feeling sinking into his bones, sucking all the warmth from his body.

Lyra shuddered and held herself, and gods, he wanted to hold her too. He wanted to pull her into his arms and cage her in them, to shield her from the world and her fears, and make her believe they would never happen.

He wouldn't let them.

He would protect her.

"He came to see me." Her fingers dug into her arms. "Evil. Cold. I've never felt such evil... such darkness."

She released her arms and held her hands out to him, her wrists close together.

"He placed new shackles on me."

That coldness became a sinking feeling, one that had his hackles rising and a need to get Lyra out of the open sweeping through him.

"He swapped them for different ones?" Grey stared at them.

She nodded. "He did it with others too. My first set of shackles were old, battered, so maybe he thought they weren't strong enough to hold me."

Or maybe the son of a bitch had been up to something.

He reached for her shackles.

She shrank away from him and he stopped and raised his eyes to hers.

"I won't hurt you. Trust me, Lyra... I just want to get a closer look." He held his hands out to her, palm up, offering her the chance to be in control.

Something flickered in her eyes, something that said she wanted him closer to her, needed him as fiercely as he needed her, but she was afraid of it.

He slowly edged his hands forwards, not wanting to startle her.

She pulled down a deep breath and moved hers towards him, and barely tensed as she settled the metal cuffs in his hands.

He was careful not to touch her bare skin as he leaned forwards and inspected the thick silver cuffs, gently turning them around her wrists. When he reached the side where the ring for the chain was, something caught his eye.

It was small and he would have missed it if the golden light of the sky hadn't highlighted it at the moment his eyes had swept over that spot.

An engraving.

He peered closer.

That cold feeling became ice in his veins.

It was an inscription.

"I don't like this at all," he whispered to her hands.

Lyra leaned over and looked at the cuffs, and then up at his face. Damn. She was close. Tempting. He dropped his eyes to her lips and then forced them back up to hers.

"There's a spell on these restraints." He pointed to the small line of words.

He couldn't understand them, but he knew a spell when he saw it, had met a travelling witch once when she had come through the pride village en route to Kincaid's castle, the old werewolf warrior who had allowed Grey's pride to make their home on his remote estate in Scotland.

"I know. It makes them flex with my form when I shift and stops me from breaking them. They could also use it to stop me from attacking them. The more important members of the group had a word they could use to freeze me for a minute… although none of them ever tried it so I'm not sure how true that part is."

Grey slowly shook his head. "I think there's more than that in this spell."

She drew her hands back towards her, and he wanted to growl as they left his and the distance between them grew again.

"What?" She looked down at the cuffs and then up at him, that fear returning to colour her eyes and make him want to hold her and tell her everything would be alright.

He crouched and checked the cuffs of the two dead females, and found a similar engraving on one of their bonds.

"Grey?" Lyra came to stand beside him again, her eyes locked on him, demanding an answer to her question.

He straightened to his full height. "I think maybe there's a tracker on them. I can't be certain… but it would explain what happened here."

"You're saying the fallen angel can hunt me using them?" She spoke slowly, a trickle of fear running through her and into him, one that made it hard for him to resist the urge to gather her into his arms and whisper promises to take away that fear.

He would protect her.

She looked at the cuffs.

"I heard the males talking once," she whispered and then her voice gained volume and confidence as her fear began to abate and she found her strength again. "It was during the march after the fallen angel had placed these cuffs on me. They mentioned another group who had caught a hellcat once but he had lost the chance to sell her when someone had attacked their auction… most of his stock had escaped, but apparently he had been furious about losing the hellcat."

Grey didn't like the sound of that at all.

"I need to find a way to get these fucking things off you." He reached for her wrists and barely stopped himself from grabbing her and trying to wrestle them off her.

That dark need to dominate her returned as his guard dropped, his fury over the thought the fallen angel might be tracking her right now, coming to take her from him, unleashing it. It goaded him into claiming her now, before it was too late.

He staggered back a step, horrified by the need that slammed into him, and that he almost wavered, almost gave into it this time, his fear of losing her giving it control over him.

He turned and stumbled a few steps away from her, each harder than the last, fighting himself with every one, desperate to place distance between them.

When he was over twenty feet from her, he couldn't move another inch, couldn't convince himself to place any more distance between him and her, or to leave her as he should.

She would be vulnerable without him near to her.

He needed to protect her.

He needed to claim her.

Gods. He tunnelled his fingers into his silver hair and gripped his head, growling as those dual needs warred inside him.

"Why do you keep doing that?" Lyra's soft voice was closer than expected, and he growled as he realised she had moved towards him.

He snapped his fangs and snarled at her, desperate to drive her away because she was tearing at his fragile control.

He couldn't take it.

He didn't want to hurt her.

She stood her ground. "It isn't because of what I've been through… it's something else. You keep pushing me away… why?"

As he lifted his head, tired and weary from fighting his instincts, he lost his grip on them and they stole control, swept through him to obliterate the part of him that wanted to keep her safe and protect her, even from himself.

He saw it in her eyes the moment she realised the answer to her question.

They widened slowly.

"Your nails are black."

CHAPTER 10

It wasn't possible.

A surge of fear had Lyra wanting to take a step backwards, away from Grey, but she planted her feet to the black dirt and refused to obey it. She had no reason to fear him. Didn't she?

It hit her hard that the male standing before her was much more than she had expected.

Much more than she had believed.

"You said you had a family... a pride... that you're a tiger... were you lying?" She couldn't bear the thought that he might have been.

Was he just like the other hellcat male, the one who had tricked her and sold her into slavery?

Had he been out to deceive her?

"No," Grey bit out, his blue eyes holding hers, an edge to them that pleaded her to believe him and not hate him.

"But hellcats are solitary."

He shook his head. "I'm not a hellcat, Lyra... I'm a tiger."

He was lying.

Now that she had seen his nails turn black, and the fires of her kind raging in his eyes, she could feel it in him.

He was a hellcat.

He stepped towards her. "I'm a tiger... but in my bloodline, there was a cross-breeding. One of my ancestors wanted to make my family stronger, so they mated with a hellcat."

Gods.

She had foolishly hoped he had been about to tell her that she had gone crazy, that everything that had happened had gotten to her and she had been imagining it.

He wasn't pure hellcat, but he had the blood of one in his veins.

"I don't understand it," he muttered to his hands as he lowered them in front of him. His silvery eyebrows furrowed and she felt a glimmer of his pain and confusion, and fear. So much fear. "I don't want to feel this way. I... I can't be around you. I'm sorry, Lyra."

He turned away from her.

Lyra stopped him with a handful of words straight from her heart.

"I need you."

She wasn't sure whether she meant she needed him to protect her from the fallen angel, or needed him physically, emotionally. It just came out, a blurted confession that only seemed to pain him.

He growled and looked back at her, his eyes vivid blue, glowing brightly in the low light, and his voice hoarse and low. "Don't say things like that. I can't…"

"I'm sorry." She risked a step towards him, the need to comfort him overwhelming her, seizing her so fiercely she couldn't stop herself from moving closer to him, even when part of her was aware she would only cause him more pain by doing so. "I didn't mean to push you."

Because he was doing his best to resist the instincts he didn't understand.

It touched her, deeper than he would ever know.

It told her how much he cared about her and how fiercely he wanted to protect her.

Because of his tiger blood, the compulsions and needs he felt were weaker, only a fraction of what he would have felt around her if he had been a full-blooded hellcat, but they were still powerful.

They were taking their toll on him.

He was bearing it for her though.

Gods, it was noble, and beautiful, of him to fight them so fiercely for her sake.

His legs gave out and his knees hit the dirt, and he bent forwards and dug his fingers into the black earth, hanging his head between his arms.

"Please, Lyra," he rasped. "I don't want to hurt you. Get away from me."

This was the reason he had left when she had spoken with the elf in the tavern, and the reason he had tried to make her leave.

This was the reason he had drawn his own blood.

He had been fighting his instincts for her.

"Go!"

Lyra shook her head even though he couldn't see it and slowly approached him. She wouldn't leave him when he was suffering because of his genes, because of her. She wanted to help him through it, needed to soothe him and assuage those instincts somehow to free him from their grip.

He was a good male.

One her heart said she could trust.

When she kneeled before him, he lifted his head and his handsome face twisted in a grimace as he growled, the pained sound tearing at that heart.

"It's okay," she whispered, her hands shaking as she thought about reaching out and placing them on his where he gripped the ground, as if he needed to anchor himself to it.

He shook his head and his eyebrows furrowed.

She managed a smile for him, even when she was falling apart inside, the sight of him hurting drawing her closer to him, filling her with a need to touch him and let him know she was here with him, and she wasn't going anywhere. He could snarl and snap at her, could try to drive her away, but she was staying right where she was.

With him.

She was going to help him through this.

Because as fiercely as she had fought it, there was no longer any denying it.

He was something to her, and she was something to him, and that was the reason his instincts had him locked in their grip, were tearing him apart with a deep need of her.

The part of her that lay damaged and broken by everything that had happened to her screamed at her to run even though this was where she wanted to be.

It sank in that she wasn't strong anymore.

She wasn't being strong by cutting herself off from the world. She wasn't being strong by keeping Grey at a distance, locked out of her heart.

She was being weak.

Being strong would be taking the risk, having the courage to try again and trust in him. It would be believing in him.

She was tired of being weak.

She wanted to be strong again.

Her eyes dropped to his full lips.

She leaned in to kiss him.

CHAPTER 11

Grey pulled his head back before Lyra could sully herself by kissing him.

"We need to keep moving." He ignored the trickle of hurt he could feel in her as he pushed onto his feet and took a step backwards, away from her, placing some much-needed distance between them.

He had no doubt in his mind now that the fallen angel was after her. The male viewed her as his prize, a replacement for a hellcat he had meant to sell but had been snatched from his grasp.

If Grey was right, and there was a tracker on her shackles, then it was only a matter of time before the male found them.

Grey was strong, but he wasn't sure he was strong enough to fight a fallen angel.

In order to protect her, he needed to get the shackles off her as soon as possible and then he would take her far from Hell, away from this wretched place and the male who was hunting her.

Dragons had been able to use magic once. It was possible one of them could read the spell and tell him what it meant, and they might be able to remove the shackles for her.

Talon would have to wait a little longer to find out what was beyond that door.

Grey was switching his mission to protecting Lyra.

Once he knew she was safe, he would come back to Hell for his brother's sake and finish what he had started.

Lyra took priority though.

She rose onto her feet, turned her back on him and started walking, her head bent and her arms wrapped around her as she trudged away from him, heading towards the dragon realm.

He deserved a little cold shoulder action he supposed.

It was for the best, even though it didn't feel as if it was, even though part of him wished Lyra had tried again to kiss him and hadn't given up so easily.

He strode after her.

She didn't look at him, didn't even acknowledge his existence, as he caught up with her. The air around her felt cold despite the heat of Hell, chilling his skin and seeping deep into his heart.

"I'll find someone to remove your restraints when we reach the dragons," he said to break the silence.

She didn't respond. She just kept walking, her eyes fixed ahead, firmly away from him.

It hurt a little.

He rubbed at the spot above his heart that stung the fiercest, trying to alleviate the pain.

Gods, he had wanted to kiss her.

Still wanted to kiss her.

She had to know that.

He hadn't meant to hurt her.

But he had.

She had shown him a sliver of trust, had been brave enough to overcome her fear and everything that had happened to her in order to touch him, to kiss him, and he had rejected her.

He scrubbed a hand over his face and shoved it through his short silver hair. He was a bastard. He glanced at her, hoping that he hadn't shaken her just as she was finding her feet again.

He kept telling himself it was better this way as they walked in silence. Maybe when they reached the village there would be a portal and a dragon who could remove her restraints, and then she could go home, far away from him.

Maybe she would find a male who deserved her, someone who could be what he couldn't for her.

Shit, but he wanted to be the only male for her.

Needed it so fiercely that he couldn't breathe as he thought of her with another. He wanted to throw his head back and roar out his fury.

He felt her eyes on him, but by the time he had looked at her, they were locked ahead of her again.

He sighed.

And caught a scent on the stifling breeze.

His focus sharpened and he closed ranks with Lyra when he sensed a powerful creature ahead of them, so he was near enough to protect her if they attacked.

High above the mountains in the distance ahead of them, a shape loomed, so large that Grey's instincts told him to go another way. Huge wings spread as the creature turned into a dive and swept downwards at breathtaking speed.

He growled and moved in front of Lyra as the dragon rocketed towards them, low to the ground, and she tensed as it flew directly overhead, a black shadow in the dim light, and wind battered them. Another snarl escaped him when the dragon wheeled around and came back, eyeing them as it made another pass, and then lazily flapped its enormous wings and banked left, heading into another valley.

As the dragon was lost from view, he grew aware of Lyra pressed close to him, her hands on his backpack, gripping it fiercely.

She was afraid.

And she had moved closer to him, trusting he would protect her.

Her hair tickled his left arm, her breath warm on his skin.

That ache started deep in his chest again, the one that demanded he turn and gather her into his arms, and kiss her this time, as she wanted to be kissed.

By him.

He slowly turned towards her and she lifted her head, her faintly glowing blue eyes meeting his, sending a shiver through him that chased away the chill and warmed his bones, and almost made him forget the reasons why he couldn't bend his head and capture those lips that called to him so sweetly.

She tipped her head up in an invitation.

The ground shook behind him, a gust of wind blasting fragments of black rock against him, and he swiftly pulled Lyra into his arms, shielding her from the sharp shards. She gasped and for a sickening heartbeat, a dreadful moment, he feared he had terrified her by touching her and she would lash out at him.

He stilled.

Rather than pushing out of his arms and attacking him for daring to touch her against her will, she burrowed deeper into his embrace, her cheek pressing against his bare chest and her hands trembling against his sides.

She didn't fear him.

She feared what had just landed behind him.

The dragon snarled and Grey growled right back at it, didn't give a shit if it was ten times his height and one hundred times more powerful than him.

He wouldn't let it near Lyra.

He looked over his shoulder at the huge black beast and pinned it with a glare he hoped conveyed every ounce of the fury pouring through his veins, a fire that commanded him to fight.

To protect Lyra.

The black dragon shook its head, long horns almost catching the muscled arch of its wings as it settled all four enormous black paws onto the dark ground. Huge talons dug into the earth, cleaving long grooves in it, and obsidian eyes dropped to him, a flare of gold and violet around its narrowed elliptical pupils.

"Fuck off," Grey snarled and gathered Lyra closer.

The immense beast cocked its head.

Lyra lifted hers and bit out something in a language he didn't know.

This time, the dragon growled, flashing fangs that were each the length of Grey's arms.

She moved backwards, out of his embrace, and held her arms up, showing them to the dragon. The beast huffed, and Grey wanted to cover her eyes when it transformed into a rugged black-haired male with midnight eyes, and scars littering his honed body. A black pair of leathers appeared on his lower half together with boots as the male strode towards them.

"Slavers?" The male looked over the silver cuffs but kept his distance.

A wise move since Grey was finding it hard to refrain from growling at the male already, the need to protect Lyra rousing his hellcat instincts and blending them into one dangerous desire to fight.

And kill.

Lyra nodded. "We thought your kind might be able to remove them."

The male rolled a thickly-muscled shoulder. "It should not prove a problem. Come... my chief will want to speak with you."

Grey didn't want to follow the male, but Lyra was moving before he could say a word, trailing behind the male but keeping her distance. He didn't trust the dragon shifter. The black-haired male looked like a warrior, and one who enjoyed fighting judging by the thick scars on his stomach and side that were still fresh and healing.

Lyra said something in the strange tongue again, the words melodic and almost magical sounding. The male grunted and pointed off to his right, across the valley to the other side.

"What are you asking?" Grey wanted to know, because as far as he knew, the Devil's domain was in that direction.

The thought of her going anywhere near such a dangerous place turned his stomach.

"Where the nearest portal is." She didn't look at him. She kept her eyes fixed on the dragon.

On his bare back.

Grey growled at that.

The black need to shove past her and attack the male, to prove himself the male more worthy of her, rose swift and fast, almost overpowering him. He growled again and clenched his teeth, curled his hands into fists and fought himself instead, struggling to tamp that need down and bring it back under control.

She was doing it on purpose, punishing him for rejecting her.

It was sheer torture.

He wrestled with his darker instincts as they trekked around the edges of a mountain and then followed a broad well-trodden path over one and into another valley. As they crested a hill on the descent, a village came into view. It was larger than he had expected.

Round stone huts filled most of the space in the valley floor, with a large clearing off to the left where dragons of all different colours milled around, some taking off and some landing. To the north of the village, an arena hugged the side of the mountain. In the centre of the village was another wide clearing, with a large building at one end of it.

A red dragon flew overhead, followed by a violet one.

Lyra bared her fangs at both of them, and a trickle of her fear ran through him, made him ache with a need to gather her back into his arms and hold her until that fear went away.

"None will hurt you... although some might fight for you." The dragon cast an emotionless, empty glance over his shoulder at her.

Grey growled at the male, making it clear that no one was going to be fighting to have Lyra as their female.

She belonged to no one.

She wrapped her arms around herself and that need to hold her grew stronger, drove him to narrow the gap between them so she would feel that he was there for her, and he wouldn't allow any dragon to attempt to stake a claim on her.

No one would own her ever again.

She was free now.

When they reached the village outskirts, it became clear that the males weren't the only ones who liked to wear only leather trousers. Females moved around the black stone huts, their colourful hair matching that of their tight leathers, their breasts unfettered and bouncing with each step they took.

Some smiled as they spotted him and flicked their long hair over their shoulders to expose their firm breasts.

An open invitation that he ignored.

These females did nothing for him.

They did something for Lyra though. She growled at every one that looked at him, and bared her fangs at those who dared to expose themselves to him in an attempt to lure him to them.

As they entered the centre of the village, and the males grew more numerous, Grey began his own growling spree. He moved closer to Lyra, trying to make it clear that she was off limits, but it didn't stop some of the males from eyeing her, an appreciative glint in their colourful gazes as they raked them over her curves, clearly imagining what they looked like beneath the baggy t-shirt and shorts.

Their dragon escort said something, pulling Grey away from a particularly vicious series of growls aimed at a handsome son of a bitch who looked as if he might cross the line and try to speak with Lyra.

The turquoise-haired male fell back and huffed as he returned his focus to the female who was fawning over him, pressing her bare breasts to his chest and swirling her fingers around his left nipple.

The stories his mother had read to him as a cub had neglected to mention that dragons were this sexually charged.

If he had known, he would have personally marched Lyra to the portal near the tavern and shoved her into it.

He wasn't sure how much more he could bear as they approached the gathering place in the village and males and females flowed out from the paths between the huts, filling the edges of the open circle.

Shit got dangerously close to going south when someone barked something in the dragon tongue and the gathered fell silent, and Grey looked at who had spoken.

A male with bright golden hair sat on an obsidian throne in front of the largest of the thatched stone huts that stood on a platform at the other end of the square, cragged black mountains rising to spear the dimly glowing sky of

Hell behind him. His large hands rested over the ornate ends of the arms of his throne, and bronze leathers hugged powerful legs that were spread wide apart.

Beside him, a female with wavy amber hair that reached her waist knelt with her head bent, her palms resting on her deep orange leather trousers. She appeared relaxed, but a sense of melancholy rolled off her.

Grey guessed from her subservient position that she belonged to the golden dragon and that it wasn't by choice.

"Brink, what cats have you dragged in with you?" the male said, a lazy drawl that made him sound calm and complacent, uncaring, when Grey's senses said he was far from it.

The male was alert, cautious, and ready to fight if needed.

The black-haired dragon dipped his head as they halted in the centre of the square. "One who is born of this realm, and has been subjugated. She seeks freedom from her shackles."

The other male eyed Lyra, golden irises bright. "I suppose we could help with that... for a price."

Grey's hackles rose.

If he meant to make Lyra pay for her freedom in any sexual way, he was going to kill the bastard. It didn't matter that he was clearly in charge of this entire clan of dragons. Grey would cleave the male's head from his neck with his bare claws.

"You have gold?"

That need to fight instantly deflated.

The way the leader's eyes brightened when he said the word 'gold' was almost comical, a clichéd reaction and need that Grey wanted to laugh at because it seemed too ridiculous to be real.

A dragon wanted gold?

The male watched him closely and Grey didn't even let a hint of a smile touch his lips.

He had the feeling that if he dared to show his amusement, it would be the last thing he did.

The dragon would crush him and eat him.

"No gold?" The male huffed. "No freedom."

"I'll get you a jewel bigger than your balls if you get me out of these shackles," Lyra snarled and the male slowly smiled.

His golden eyes twinkled at her. "I have big balls."

She planted her hands on her hips. "I don't doubt it. I have a big jewel. A sapphire. It was my mother's. She stole it when she escaped my father. If you get these off me, I'll go through the portal to my home and I'll come back with it."

"Brink, Tanix and Eyrie will go with you."

The black-haired male obediently stepped forwards. A large male with pale blue hair tied in a thong at the nape of his neck and icy eyes broke from the guards on the left of the dais. From the ones on the right, an equally muscled male with forest-green short hair, jade eyes and a jagged scar that ran diagonally across his chest from his left shoulder to his right hip moved to meet with the blue-haired one in front of their alpha, and then marched forwards at his side to halt next to Brink.

The trio were formidable.

Lyra's pulse beat a little quicker, and Grey edged towards her, wanting her to know that he was here with her.

"Not a wise idea." She kept her eyes on the male in charge as he pushed onto his feet. His handsome face darkened and his eyes glowed brighter. She held her hands up in front of her, palms facing him. Trying to calm him. "I live in the mortal realm."

The male looked from her to Grey.

Grey shrugged. "Norway, apparently."

A murmur ran through the crowd gathered around them, and Lyra's heartbeat ticked up, her fear returning as she looked at all the dragons.

He moved another step closer to her, and she looked over her shoulder at him, that fear he had sensed in her shining in her blue eyes. He silently told her that she would be fine, he would get those shackles off her and get her away from the dragons, and he would see her home.

"I'll stay while she gets the jewel." He stepped past her, stealing the golden-haired male's attention. "I have business in the dragon realm. I can look into it while she goes to retrieve the jewel. Your men can escort me."

The leader stared at him, and Grey could see his mind working, churning as he considered the offer, his golden eyes still glowing brightly.

He really wanted that jewel.

"Fine," the male snapped, raised his hand and two females approached Lyra, a pretty blonde and one with lilac hair. "Take her to the smith."

Grey watched the females as they fell in beside Lyra and ushered her towards the right side of the village. When she looked back at him, he saw the need in her eyes and felt it echo in his heart, and he went to follow her as she wanted.

"Male," the leader barked, halting him in his tracks. He turned back towards him. "You have a name?"

"Grey." He looked from the male to Lyra, and had to pull down a slow breath to calm himself when she disappeared from view.

Gods, he needed to find her.

He needed to see her.

This distance between them was too much.

He had to know where she was, needed eyes on her at all times, needed to see she was alright and unharmed. Safe.

"My name is Ren. You mentioned you have business here. This is my domain and I will know what business it is you have in it." The male eased back down onto his throne. "Speak and tell me."

The one called Brink urged him forwards, and Grey resisted, stood his ground and continued to stare in the direction Lyra had gone.

He did have business in the dragon realm, but that business was Lyra now. He didn't care what Archangel were up to, and he wouldn't, not until she was safe and far from this hellish land, and the male pursuing her.

"Speak, or I will have the female brought back here and new shackles placed on her."

Grey snarled and bared his fangs at Ren. The male held his gaze, unflinching in the face of his fury, his golden eyes placid and betraying nothing.

Brink shoved him hard in his back, forcing him to stumble forwards across the black dirt.

Grey tore his eyes away from the path Lyra had taken and approached the platform where Ren sat, locking gazes with him. If it would stop the male from threatening Lyra, then he would do as the male bid and tell him why he had come to Hell.

He stopped just short of the platform and looked up at Ren.

"I'm hunting Archangel scouts."

Ren's eyes darkened and his pupils narrowed, beginning to turn elliptical. He knew Archangel then, and he didn't like them judging by the anger that laced his scent.

A few of the people in the crowd lining the square began whispering to each other.

Brink lowered one hand to his stomach and clutched it, his skin paling as he stared off into the distance. Had an Archangel hunter given him the wound behind the dark pink scar he held?

Ren snarled and stood sharply and everyone fell silent again, some of them shrinking back, as if they feared him.

Grey wouldn't blame them if they did.

The male cut an imposing figure as he stood on his dais, his golden hair catching the warm breeze and the fires of Hell glowing in his eyes, and every muscle of his near seven-foot frame tensed.

Only the amber-haired female showed no outward sign of fear. She remained kneeling beside his throne, motionless and calm. Either she had balls of steel, or she had slipped away from the world in order to cope with what was happening to her.

The sight of her stirred a dark and dangerous need in Grey's blood, a deep desire to free her from her invisible shackles.

If he dared to try, he wouldn't survive, and she would no doubt be punished by Ren.

Besides, one of the guards stationed at the left side of the dais, a male with bright silver hair and deep silver leathers, couldn't keep his mercury-coloured eyes off her. Whenever Ren was distracted, whenever the alpha had an outburst that shook everyone but her, those mercury eyes slipped to her, watched her.

Watched over her.

It looked as if it was only a matter of time before she found her freedom.

The male wore the same look Grey felt sure he did at times, a yearning he couldn't contain and a need he fought a losing battle to deny. He wanted the female, and he would move Hell, Earth and Heaven to have her.

"Mortals," Ren spat and narrowed his eyes on Grey. "What know you of them? Fiends from this Archangel came to my lands recently and bewitched one of my warriors, stole the females my warriors had taken as their war prizes, and now another of my males has gone missing."

And Ren wanted war.

Brink growled from beside Grey, "I have seen them... scouting parties as you said. There are many of them, with much strange technology."

"Where?" Grey turned to the black-haired male.

Sparks of violet flickered in his midnight eyes.

Ren loosed a low snarl. Brink turned to face him.

"I returned to report this, and found these felines approaching our home."

Grey didn't like the way Brink said that, because it sounded a lot like he was insinuating he and Lyra were involved with Archangel in some way, and were a threat to the dragons.

"I need to know where they are. Research we uncovered when we broke into their building—" Grey started.

"You have been in their home?" Ren interjected and took a step towards him. "Speak of it and what you know."

Brink stared at him.

Hard.

When Grey glanced at the male, his eyes were brighter, more purple than black, but they were unfocused, fixed on him but not seeing him.

"They all smell the same," he murmured, voice a bare whisper. "They all smell of..."

"Brink!" Ren barked and the black-haired dragon snapped out of it and dazedly looked at his leader.

He immediately lowered his head. "My apologies. I must have drifted away."

Or lost himself entirely in some sort of trance.

Tanix and Eyrie eyed him closely, their brows furrowed with deep lines as they frowned, jaws set like steel vices. They didn't trust Brink. Because he was different to them, afflicted by something?

"What were we talking about?" Brink said.

"The mortals." Ren cast his fellow dragon a concerned look that lasted only a second, was quickly replaced with a mask that concealed his feelings.

While Tanix and Eyrie didn't trust Brink, their alpha clearly did, and had a soft spot for the dark dragon.

Brink's black eyebrows knitted hard and he dropped his gaze to the ground. "I have seen them in a few areas now… always close to the portals. I have the feeling they are using fae to get them through."

That didn't sound good.

It matched what Grey had read in the reports Talon had shown him though. There had been several projects that mentioned employing fae or people capable of working the portals to get them through the pathways from the mortal realm into Hell.

"The first group I spotted were the largest party. They had set up camp a day's march south from here."

"How long ago was this?" Grey didn't dare hope the date would match what had been listed in the project he was researching for Talon.

Brink frowned, and then lifted his head and met Grey's gaze. "Almost a lunar cycle ago now."

Gods.

It had to be the same team.

Ren came to the edge of the platform. "These are the ones you are hunting?"

Grey nodded.

The golden-haired male stared him down, his eyes impassive and cold. "Then while your female retrieves the gem I was promised as payment for removing her shackles, you will pay the price of her freedom."

He snarled at Ren, baring his emerging fangs, and flexed his fingers as his claws extended. No fucking way this dragon was going to lay a hand on her. He would kill the son of a bitch before it could happen.

Brink's hand came down hard on his shoulder, black claws digging into his bare skin as he gripped it, and Grey hissed and tried to shake him off.

"Swear my payment to me," Ren's eyes slid towards the path Lyra had taken, "Or the female will be mine and I will make her watch as I slit you open."

A cold blade met the front of his throat.

Brink lifted it, forcing Grey to tip his head up to avoid being cut, making him look up at Ren where he loomed over him, a glimmer of darkness in his eyes that warned he would do it.

He was no use to Lyra dead, and there was no way he would let this male touch her.

He growled at the bastard.

"What do you want me to do?"

CHAPTER 12

Lyra couldn't remember how it had felt to have nothing around her wrists, no metal weighing her down or spell sapping her strength. Had it always felt like this?

She stared at her stained naked wrists as she walked through the dragon village, fascinated with them. They felt light, strangely so, and she could feel her strength returning, simmering just below the surface of her skin.

Shit, it felt good.

She wanted to show Grey.

There was a bounce in her step as she headed towards the centre of the village, put there by picturing how Grey's pale blue eyes would light up with warmth and relief when he saw her shackles were gone and she was finally free.

Able to move on with her life.

Her steps slowed, the light that had been filling her fading as she entered the square and spotted Grey.

A beautiful female stood before him, her long crimson hair barely concealing her naked breasts, her red lips curved in a wide alluring smile as she spoke with him.

He said something back to her.

The corners of his lips curved.

Pain lanced Lyra's heart and she took a step back, her hands falling to brush her thighs as she stared across the open space at Grey, watched him talking with the female. He wasn't pushing her away, not as he had pushed Lyra away when she had tried to be close to him, had dared to risk everything all so she could kiss him.

He looked as if he might welcome it if the dragon offered her lips.

A vision of him dipping his head to kiss the female leaped into her mind and she couldn't shut it out, even as it tore at her, ripped down that strength that had been flowing back into her and left her battered, weak all over again.

She backed off another step.

She knew about dragons. They bedded whoever caught their eye, scratched their itches wherever and whenever they could, and had no qualms about taking multiple partners whenever the mood struck them.

The female laughed, her eyes lighting up with it, and reached out to place her hand on Grey's chest.

Lyra shook her head and stumbled back another step as the need to fight poured through her, had a growl curling from her lips and her claws extending before she could stop them.

No. She didn't want to fight.

She didn't want to fight for Grey.

Because he didn't want her.

She forced herself to turn her back on him and walk away, but it was hard, her movements slower than she would have liked as her hellcat instincts pushed her to remain, to destroy the dragon who had dared to try to steal what was hers.

Grey belonged to her.

No. No he didn't. He never would. She could see that now. She could see what a fool she had been to think anything could happen between them.

"Lyra."

The sound of him calling her name shattered the hold her hellcat instincts had on her, freeing her from their chains, and she broke into a dead run, weaving through the huts and heading away from him as quickly as she could manage.

She didn't dare look back as she sprinted towards the mountains, feared that she would stop if she saw him coming after her, or that he would break her heart by not being there.

That mocking voice whispered he would remain with the beauty he had been smiling at, the one he clearly wanted.

Her left leg ached but she kept running, didn't slow even when she hit the foothills of the mountain. She scrambled up the loose rock, the sharp black stones cutting into her palms and her feet, and breathed hard as she reached what looked like a path.

She followed it, the ache in her leg becoming a dull throb that had her wincing with each step. It slowed her down and she cursed it as she rubbed her thigh and walked as swiftly as she could manage. She would rest when she was far enough away that the vision of Grey with that female no longer taunted her.

The black dragon had said the portal was this way.

Maybe she could reach it without stopping for a break and then she would be almost home.

She could forget about Grey.

Gods, the thought of him with another female was sheer torment, up there with the pain the slavers had put her through. She couldn't handle it. She tried to shut it out, but it persisted, stabbed at her heart as she stumbled and tripped along the path, desperate to get away.

With every step she managed, the visions grew more heated, the images of the dragon female touching and stroking Grey, pressing her lips to his flesh and tasting him as Lyra wanted, and him welcoming it from the bitch, torturing her.

Her hellcat side flared up again, prowled beneath her skin and pushed her to turn back around, go back down the mountain, find the redhead and rip her to shreds.

If the female was dead, Grey would no longer want her.

Lyra staggered left as her leg gave out, hit a boulder hard and sagged against it, breathing rapidly. Her heart raced, sweat trickling down her spine, and she grimaced and growled as the throbbing in her leg grew more intense. She welcomed the pain, because it broke the hold the visions had on her, giving her a reprieve from them for a heartbeat.

She tried to push onto her feet.

Her legs buckled.

Strong arms grabbed her and a male growled in her right ear.

"What the fuck do you think you're doing running off like that?"

Grey.

A very angry Grey.

The relief that swept through her stole more of her strength, utterly shattered that vision of him with another female and let light pour back into her heart.

He had come for her.

He had left the other female behind in order to be with her.

He huffed and righted her, and then he was gone, pacing away from her. She lifted her eyes to him and weathered the growl he directed at her, and the fierce flash of fangs. His pale blue eyes glowed brightly, his pupils enormous in their centres, and his bare chest heaved as he paced, breathing hard and fast.

She could feel his fury, his anger.

His distress.

He shoved his hands through his silver hair, growled as he bent forwards, and then threw his head back and roared.

She tensed, her heart leaping high into her throat and lodging there. There was so much pain in that roar, agony she had caused.

He lowered his hands to his sides, exhaled hard and stared at her, an empty expression on his face. His eyes spoke to her though, relayed his hurt and his despair.

"How the fuck am I meant to protect you when you run away from me?" He looked down at her hands. "Or is it that you don't need me anymore now that your restraints are gone?"

Gods, no. It was nothing like that.

"What am I supposed to do?" she bit out, his anger fuelling hers, together with the vision of him that haunted her, the sight of him smiling at another female when he wouldn't smile at her.

When he didn't want her.

"If I had stayed…" She looked away from him, not wanting to say it, not willing to risk herself again like that.

He laughed, the sound mocking and cold. "I understand. I do… it's not the first time it's happened to me… and it's for the best."

She had no damned clue what he was talking about, but she didn't like that despondent edge to his deep voice, or the resigned look in his eyes.

"It's for the best that I want to kill any female who so much as looks at you?" she snapped. "I suppose females getting upset when you look at another female is an every day occurrence for you then?"

His eyes widened.

He stared at her, his silence slowly destroying her confidence, pulling apart the strength she had mustered and making her squirm.

Damn. She shouldn't have said that. She should have just walked away.

But she couldn't.

She couldn't walk away from him.

She had run, but all the while she had been aware that she wouldn't leave him, that she would stop eventually and she would turn back.

Because she needed him.

She had never needed anyone the way she needed Grey.

He was everything to her.

"I was just trying to get information," he said, his tone calm and even now, no trace of anger in it. No trace of any emotion. She could sense his wariness as he studied her, holding himself at a distance from her. His eyes narrowed. "I'm not interested in that female, and what's it to you if I am? The last I checked, I wasn't yours… and you didn't want to be mine."

She averted her gaze, stared off up the path to her left, and struggled to find the right words to say, the ones that wouldn't leave her completely exposed and vulnerable.

The ones that wouldn't hurt him.

She wasn't sure how many times she had cursed male hellcats in front of him, but clearly it had been enough times to leave a mark on him and now he foolishly thought she didn't want him.

She had tried to kiss him for gods' sakes.

He took a slow, measured step towards her. "What's it to you?"

She could feel his need to know the answer to that question, but she couldn't say it.

He lifted his hand, and she held her ground when he hesitated, remained still as he struggled with himself, and a sliver of his fear ran through her veins. He was afraid this would be too much for her. It wouldn't. She wanted to tell him that. She wasn't fragile, liable to break if he touched her.

She would welcome it.

His palm gently cupped her cheek, his touch so soft and light that it completely undid her, stripping away her strength and leaving her weak, trembling inside.

She didn't resist him when he applied a little pressure, enough to draw her head around to face him.

She tentatively raised her eyes to his.

Hell, they were tender as they searched hers, filled with warmth and need, a desire to know all the things she wanted to keep hidden from him.

"It's no use hiding from me, Lyra," he rasped, his voice thick and low, stirring heat in her veins as he stepped closer. "I can feel you."

She closed her eyes, needing to shut him out again, but she couldn't. He was in now, and he was in deep, way past the barrier around her heart, beyond the point where she could push him back out, not without hurting him.

Not without hurting herself.

"You're upset," he husked, a bare whisper, and leaned closer, brought his forehead to her right temple and rested it there.

She trembled at the feel of him so close to her and wrestled with the instincts that told her to lean into him, to move closer still, to tilt her head just a fraction of a degree and bring their lips into contact. She was sure he would kiss her then. He wouldn't be able to resist her.

He would give her what she needed.

All of him.

She needed that with a ferocity that shook her, roused her hellcat side and had her verging on taking hold of him.

And never letting go.

His breath was warm on her skin, his enticing scent swirling around her, and that heat that always seemed to roll off him called to her, begging her to step into his arms and let him hold her too.

He murmured, "Gods... do you think it doesn't upset me too when males look at you? Do you think it doesn't drive me mad when you speak with them?"

His fingers twitched against her face, tense for a second before he dropped his hand from her cheek and turned away, breaking contact with her.

"I'm sorry."

She grabbed his right wrist before he could pull away from her again, refusing to let him go this time.

She wouldn't make the same mistake twice.

She wouldn't let him escape.

"Don't apologise," she said and he tensed, his bare shoulders going rigid, but remained with his back to her. She pulled down a deep breath for courage, and put it all out there, because one of them needed to make their feelings clear. "You're right. I can't stand you looking at other females... because I want you all to myself."

He finally looked over his shoulder at her, his striking blue eyes meeting hers, filled with incredulity and disbelief. "You really mean that?"

Lyra nodded, a little afraid of where things were going. It felt as if it was happening so quickly, even when the build-up had been long, and a touch infuriating at times.

The soft edge his eyes gained told her that he wasn't going to use it against her, reminded her that with him, she didn't need to be strong all the time. She didn't need to guard herself so fiercely.

She could let him in and trust him.

"Why?"

That whispered question broke something inside her, tore at her heart as his blue eyes darted between hers, and his emotions swept through their fragile link, relaying everything to her.

All of his hurt.

His fear.

She frowned. "Why not?"

He tugged free of her grip and paced away from her, past his backpack that lay discarded on the trail, and only stopped when he reached the point where the path began to slope downwards into the dragon clan's valley.

"I'm not exactly a prize," he said to that valley, his back to her, his voice distant. "You can do better."

Lyra's frown deepened. What had gotten into him?

She had thought he had been keeping his distance because he either didn't want to frighten her or because he didn't want her.

But as she stared at his rigid back, and sifted through the emotions she could feel flowing through him, she got the impression it ran deeper than that.

He honestly believed he was unworthy of her.

"Is this because I'm a hellcat?" She wasn't sure why it would be. It wasn't as if hellcats were held in particularly high regard by the other feline shifter species.

He tilted his head slightly towards her, barely enough that he could see her out of the corner of his eye, and slowly shook his head. "It's because…"

His silver eyebrows knitted hard and he angled his head downwards, away from her.

No damn way he was getting away with leaving her hanging like that.

She had bared part of herself for him.

She had let him in.

It was time he did the same for her.

She had half a mind to make him answer her, but the fear that flowed through him stole her voice and her breath. What was he thinking to make himself feel so afraid, so unsure and so hurt?

Whatever it was, it was cutting at him.

Deeply.

She pushed away from the boulder, her legs stronger from her rest, and turned towards him, but remained at a distance, giving him time and space, because she could feel how much he needed it. He was trying to fight the feelings, to muster the courage to finish what he had started to say.

"Grey," she whispered and he lowered his head further, but the feelings that she could sense in him shifted, the fear fading a little. Because she had spoken to him, had said his name gently with every drop of the affection that she held for him? "I need to know why you feel I can do better than you. I want to understand you, Grey. Please don't shut me out."

She risked a step towards him.

"Don't, Lyra." It came out hoarse, strained to the point of breaking, and her heart bled for him. "Please?"

She couldn't do as he had asked. He was hurting, and she needed to take that pain away.

She closed the distance between them and didn't hesitate. She took hold of his hand, slipping her fingers through the gap between his thumb and his palm, and stepped around him, so she could see his face.

Gods.

The pain in his blue eyes stole her breath.

It echoed in her heart.

What had happened to the gorgeous warrior with a heart of steel who had saved her and the others from the hell of slavery?

What had happened to the powerful, confident male who was on a mission and wouldn't let anything stand in his way?

She raised her hand and he edged backwards.

"Don't touch me. I don't… I can't…" He closed his eyes and his voice dropped to a whisper. "If you knew what I was—"

His head snapped up, his eyes meeting hers.

"It was foolish of me to let things carry on this long, and I haven't been honest with you… but I will now." Those beautiful blue eyes gained a wild edge. "I need this over with because I can't bear it anymore. I can't bear lying to you… fooling myself into thinking you'll look at me the same way once you know what I am."

Lyra didn't like the sound of that.

He broke away from her and fumbled with his black trousers, his hands shaking violently as he undid the button and dealt with the zipper. She moved back a step to avoid being hit by a boot as he toed them off and kicked them aside.

She caught a glimpse of him in all of his glory as he shoved his trousers down and then he had shifted.

She stared at the large animal in front of her.

Unsure what she was meant to see in him that he found so appalling, that he thought would put her off him and make her despise him for some reason.

Unsure what he had been lying about.

All she saw before her was a beautiful, breathtaking, white tiger.

Soulful blue eyes held hers, and then he lowered his head and turned it away from her a little, and his shame blasted through her, the depth of it startling her and bringing tears to her eyes as she realised what he had meant.

Gods, he thought there was something wrong with him because he had come out purest white and black.

Her beautiful male.

She went to him, eased to her knees in front of him and took hold of his cheeks in both of her palms. His white fur was soft against her skin, his whiskers tickling her forearms as she forced him to look at her.

It was all there in his eyes.

The hurt. The shame. The fear.

All this time they had been together, he had been thinking she would reject him the moment she had seen him in his tiger form.

It broke her heart.

The tears lining her lashes slipped down her cheeks.

She looked at him, trying to find fault in him and finding none at all. What should have been amber on him was snow white, reminding her of home, and his black stripes had an inky blue sheen as they caught the light, no doubt a product of his hellcat genes.

"You're beautiful," she whispered, voice a little hoarse as she fought the tears that kept coming. Tears that were for him, because someone had made him believe there was something wrong with him. Fuck, she wanted to hunt them down and kill them, wanted to make them suffer as he did. She stroked her fingers through his thick fur. "I've never seen a tiger as beautiful as you are. You're incredible. You had me worried there for a moment… I thought you were going to transform into a wholly different creature."

He tried to look away from her, and she lowered her right hand to beneath his broad chin and kept his eyes on her. He never had to be ashamed around her. Never. He was far more majestic than she had expected. Far more beautiful. If she had to tell him that every day of his life in order to make him believe her, then she would gladly do it.

"I don't understand what your problem is," she murmured.

And gasped when he suddenly shifted back.

He knelt before her, his head bent, silver hair falling down against his forehead and blue eyes fixed on the black dirt between them. "I'm a freak."

Lyra stroked his cheek, running her fingers over the sculpted perfection of his cheekbones down to the strong defined line of his jaw. "You're unique."

"I came out wrong," he bit out.

The pain in him increased.

"Gods, I fucking hate whoever made you feel that way," she snarled and he tensed, his eyes leaping to meet hers, filled with surprise and a touch of awe, before they dropped to his knees. "Was it your family?"

He was quick to shake his head.

"Tiger society… it… our markings are celebrated. They're the pride of our species."

She could see where this was going.

"They're just jealous." She settled her palm against his cheek. "You're more beautiful than they are and they can't stand it."

She never had been able to understand the mindset of people who treated others poorly purely because they were different to them. Everyone was different and that was what should have been celebrated. The tigers were stupid for celebrating everyone looking like a clone of each other.

"I wish I came out like my twin. I wish I was normal." He closed his eyes.

No way he was shutting her out.

"What's so great about looking like everyone else? Why would you want to look like your brother… why would you want to be someone else, Grey?" She smoothed her hand over his cheek. "When you shifted, all I saw was a beautiful tiger, made all the more beautiful by your distinct markings. When I look at you now, I see you. I see the male who saved me, who loves his brother so fiercely he's trekking halfway across Hell for his sake, and one who wants to protect his pride even though they've clearly been treating him badly. Personally, I would have left them long ago."

She sighed and lowered her hand to his jaw, and eased his head up. He still didn't look at her.

"You didn't. You had a mission to protect your sister, and you stuck with it, even though the pride were cruel to you. The freaks are the ones who treated you badly just because you are different to them, when they should have seen past your markings to the male beneath." She dropped her hand to his bare chest. "They should have seen the heart that beats inside you, full of love and a strong desire to protect."

She lifted her eyes to his as they opened to her and stared deep into them.

"They should have seen the beautiful male I do."

CHAPTER 13

Grey couldn't breathe as he stared into Lyra's tranquil blue eyes and saw the truth shining in them.

She honestly thought he was beautiful.

She had seen all of him, and she hadn't found him wanting, hadn't found him disgusting. She hadn't left him.

If anything, she had moved closer to him.

The anger he could feel in her touched him as deeply as her words about him, gave them strength that made him believe her. She wanted to fight his pride, wanted to hurt those who had wounded him, and she wanted to do it for his sake.

Gods, he couldn't bear it.

His female was just too wonderful.

He slid his hand around the nape of her neck beneath her black hair, pulled her towards him and claimed her lips. She gasped into his mouth, a moan following it as she leaned into him and began to return the kiss. The soft sweep of her lips across his drove him wild, but tamed him at the same time, helped him keep control of himself when he wanted to kiss her hard, fiercely bruising her lips with it, desperation driving him.

He kissed her as softly, as slowly, as he could manage, his heart thundering against his ribs, nerves threatening to get the better of him as his body reacted to her taste, her warmth, and how soft her lips were beneath his.

She rose on her knees, forcing him to tip his head back and follow her, and her hands claimed his shoulders, the heat of them searing him as she moved closer still. Her tongue probed his lips and he opened for her, groaned as her tongue met his, all warmth and silky wetness, and her taste flooded him.

He couldn't get enough.

He planted his hands on her hips.

She gasped and he tensed, snatched them away again, fear he had hurt her lancing his heart, stabbing deep like a knife.

She broke away from his lips, pressed her forehead against his and whispered against his lips, "Gods, don't be gentle with me. Don't hold back… because I can't."

He hissed and groaned as she raked short claws over his shoulders and down his back, dropped her lips to his throat and kissed it, licked and nipped at it. He tensed, every inch of his body going rigid.

She kissed downwards, pushing him back as she did, and he breathed hard as he planted his hands behind him to stop himself from falling over. A little moan escaped her as she feathered her fingers over his chest, over the pronounced ridges of his muscles, and lifted her eyes to his, her mouth still close to his skin. She bit her lip and pressed her nails in, and he groaned and shuddered as fire swept through him, rushed down his torso to his balls and cranked them tight.

"Gods," he breathed and trembled as she lowered her hungry gaze to the juncture of his thighs.

Did she like what she saw?

He was so hard for her, painful and throbbing with need, feared he might explode if she so much as breathed on him. Her moan was his answer, had another shiver tripping through him, lighting up his senses and stirring his hunger to dizzying new heights.

Fuck, he had never been so hard.

She kissed down his chest, stealing his focus away from her hands, and from his fears as he lost himself in her again, in the way shivers of pleasure tripped through him whenever she licked or teased him with a fang.

Her hand wrapped around his shaft.

Grey barked and his hips launched forwards, the touch so unexpected he didn't have a chance to contain the reaction.

His cheeks heated when she lifted her head, locking eyes with him, hers filled with surprise.

For a heart-stopping moment, he feared she would pull away, would leave him after all.

Would find herself a more experienced male to satisfy that need he could sense in her.

She launched at him and her lips seized his, claws pressing deep into his shoulders as she kissed him so hard he couldn't keep up with her desperate movements. She raked her nails down his chest and he growled into her mouth as he shivered, a hunger to fight her rising inside him, the pain pushing him to master the wildcat going to war on him.

When he claimed command of the kiss, his left hand tunnelling into her hair to hold her against his lips, she moaned and shook, nipped at his lips and pushed him harder still. He growled, twisted her hair in his hand, locking her in place, and deepened the kiss, thrusting his tongue past her lips to tangle with hers.

That need to make her submit to him returned, stronger than before.

He broke away from her lips and breathed through it, refusing to let it master him. He wouldn't do that to Lyra.

It seemed she had no qualms about doing it to him.

He grunted when his back slammed into the dirt and stared at her. She swiftly straddled him, her hands planted against his chest, her blue eyes glowing as she stared down at him, the hunger in them calling to him, demanding he satisfy it.

That trickle of fear broke through again, tried to tangle him in vines and make him choke.

Lyra didn't give it a chance.

She worked her body against his, rubbing his rigid shaft, the friction driving him mad, dragging his hunger for her back to the fore and obliterating his fears.

He needed her.

She bent over him, her hair tickling his bare skin as she kissed downwards. His breath hitched.

He craned his neck and stared at her as she travelled lower, all of him going still as she kissed over his stomach, swirled her tongue around his navel, and kept on going.

Sweet gods.

She flicked her tongue over the head of his cock.

His hips jerked, length bobbing hard in response, and he grunted and clawed at the dirt. He shook his head, pleading her not to do that again. Everything they had done so far had almost been too much for him. He wasn't sure he could bear her placing her mouth on him.

The wicked look in her eyes said that she wasn't going to let him find release in that way.

She couldn't.

He focused on her, groaned as he felt the need inside her, one that had grown the moment she had realised he was new to this.

She hungered for him.

Wanted him inside her.

Just the thought had him on the verge of spilling.

"Fuck, Lyra, drive me crazy again." Because she had done it on purpose the first time, knew the way to tap into his instincts and make him wild for her, out of control.

She knew how to push him to a place where fear didn't exist, where he didn't think, he just acted. He needed to go there, because he wanted to do this with her, and he wanted it to be good for her. He was sure he could manage that if she just gave him a little push.

She rose onto her feet.

He stared at her as she slowly undid the belt on her shorts, his breath hitching as she eased the fly open and shimmied out of them. His eyes followed them as they dropped to her feet and she stepped out of them.

He tracked up her legs and swallowed hard as he reached the apex of them, covered by her black t-shirt.

Lyra eased the hem up.

Revealing a neat thatch of black curls that glistened in the low light.

He growled and was on her in a flash, a slave to his need to know how she tasted there. She gasped as her back hit the boulder and he pressed her against it, seared her with a kiss that had her clawing at him again. His cock met her warm slick flesh and he shuddered, his need to taste her forgotten.

He thrust slowly, rubbing himself through her cleft, groaning as his legs weakened. "Oh gods."

Lyra lifted her legs and looped them around his hips.

He stared down at her where she lay on the boulder, her eyes on his face, hooded and dark with need.

Grey lowered his eyes to his hips, groaned and shuddered as he watched his cock sliding through her flesh, glistening with her juices. Oh fucking gods. He swallowed hard, planted his trembling hands against the boulder on either side of her waist, and lost himself a little in how mesmerising it was to watch his hard length rubbing against her.

"Grey," she murmured, a desperate plea that tugged at him.

His female needed him.

She couldn't take much more.

He wanted to feel her climax around him.

He took hold of his rigid cock in his shaking left hand, and drank her sweet moan as he rubbed the blunt head downwards.

"*Grey.*"

She arched her back, thrusting her breasts up into the air.

He groaned and shifted his cock a little lower.

Her left hand shot to his, gripping his right forearm like a vice, squeezing his bones until a dull ache throbbed in them, and she threw her other hand above her head, grasping the back of the boulder.

He breathed hard, struggling to settle his racing heart as he found her slick opening. He nudged his hips forwards, moaned and shook as he edged inside her, as he watched his cock disappearing into her beautiful body.

Oh, dear fucking gods.

His right hand tightened against the boulder, entire body tensing as he eased forwards, sank deeper into her wet welcoming heat, eliciting a low soft moan from her as she dug her nails into his arm.

"Oh... gods." She sounded like him.

Did it feel as good to her, as mind-blowing, as it did to him?

He wanted to look at her face, but he couldn't tear his eyes away from his cock as he kept inching into her. When he hit an obstruction, he looked up at her.

"I think you're a bit big," she murmured, breathless and trembling.

"I'm hurting you." He went to pull out and she gripped his arm tighter, so tight his bones ached.

"You *dare* stop now." Her blue eyes flashed at him. "Gods, I need you."

He growled low in his throat at that, at the thought this beautiful female wanted him that fiercely, would fight him if he tried to stop.

Would seek to master him.

She moaned, tipped her head back and dragged her t-shirt up with her free hand, exposing the flat plane of her stomach and the curves of her breasts.

Their dark rosy tips puckered, calling to him. He wanted to taste them too. He wanted to hear her moan as he sucked and tugged on them, as he rolled them between his teeth and pinched them.

Grey ran his eyes down over her curves, to the point where he was joined with her. Her legs tightened against his back and he groaned as her hips lifted and he sank a little deeper, another inch into her.

He placed his hands on her knees where they were locked against his hips, and skimmed his palms down her thighs, and up her sides. He pressed his thumbs into her stomach, savouring the way she felt around him, and beneath his touch, and the connection that blossomed between them.

Stealing his breath.

She pressed her heels against his backside.

Trying to control him again.

He snarled, bared his fangs at her and gripped her hip with his left hand, holding her in place and stopping her from moving. He withdrew a few inches, groaned at the sight of his cock glistening with her arousal, and plunged back in. She moaned, her back arching in response.

He did it again, a longer stroke this time, pulling out enough that he could almost see the head of his cock before driving back into her, making her feel every inch of him and how hard she made him, how much he needed her.

She gripped his arm again and pushed her t-shirt up higher with her other hand. The sight of her fondling her breasts tore another growl from his lips.

He released her hip and planted his hand against the boulder again as he began driving into her, each slow curl of his hips pulling him almost all the way out before he thrust back in. The sight of her teasing her own breasts had him forgetting watching his cock, had him locked on her and how erotic she looked.

He wanted to touch them too.

He growled as he leaned over her, dropping to his right elbow as he claimed her hip with his left hand again to hold her in place. She moaned and gave him a wicked little smile as she hooked her hand around the back of his neck and traced her fingers over his nape.

He shuddered and thrust deeper, harder, a shiver tripping down his spine to his balls as she teased the sensitive spot with her claws.

Damn.

He grunted and his face screwed up.

Her nails raked harder, had the scent of his blood filling the air and his hips faltering as another need hijacked his body, stealing control.

He wanted to bite her nape.

His fangs extended, his nails turning black as he pressed them into her hip and hooked his right hand around her shoulder, holding her in place beneath him. She moaned as he thrust harder, body rolling beneath him, hips countering his thrusts as she rode him, pushing him a little harder. He groaned and eyed her neck, lost himself in thoughts of sinking his fangs into her sweet flesh and claiming her.

Binding them as mates.

The urge to flip her on her front and take her from behind while he plunged his fangs into her nape was powerful, almost overwhelming him.

"Grey." Her soft voice pulled him back to her.

Blue eyes met his, understanding dancing among the hunger in them, no trace of anger over the desire she had sensed in him, or any amount of fear.

She lured him down to her and kissed him, and he groaned as he pumped her harder, poured all of his need into making love with her, into giving her a release that would satisfy her, and him both.

She wasn't ready for that leap yet.

Maybe one day.

The thought that she might be his eternally, that she might bind herself to him, ripped at his strength and had him slowing his kiss, savouring her as she gave herself to him. She moaned against his lips and kissed him softly.

Gods, he didn't deserve her.

But he had the feeling she was his.

He would cherish her forever.

He curled his hips, used her moans as a guide as he filled her, stretching her tight body around his cock. His balls drew up and he gritted his teeth, focused on the pain to hold back his own release. It was impossible.

She felt too good, and he was too far gone.

He grunted as release boiled up his cock, as his body gave a hard kick that sent a wave of warmth through him. He throbbed inside her, groaning with each jet of his seed, trembling as he marked her as his, gave her every drop.

She wrought more from him as she tightened around him, her moans filling his ears, and pushed him back, so he was stood over her, his hands against the rock beneath her.

He dazedly watched as she lowered her hand to her flesh and teased her pert nub with her fingers.

He wanted to do that for her.

He wanted to make her climax.

He replaced her fingers with his own, brushing them swiftly across her bead as she had been, his cock still lodged deep in her core.

"Oh, Grey," she whispered, her breaths coming faster as she arched her back again, thrusting her bare breasts into the air.

He rubbed her harder, faster, watched her face as it screwed up and she bit her lip. She tensed, growing tighter around him, ripping a grunt from his lips.

That grunt became a moan of sheer pleasure as she cried out and her entire body jerked, her core quivering and throbbing around his shaft, and fire swept through him in response, had him joining her as a second release crashed over him. She moaned and wriggled her hips, and he kept up his assault with his fingers as he pressed his cock deeper inside her. Fuck. He pulsed harder as her body gripped and milked him.

She was close again.

He could feel it, that desperate need to find another release that was just beyond her reach.

He pulled out of her, dropped to his knees and placed his mouth on her. She bucked up and moaned as he thrust two fingers into her, their combined releases running down his hand and arm. He sucked at her nub, swirling his tongue around it and flicking it as he stroked her with his fingers, sending her soaring higher.

Closer.

Gods, she tasted sweet. Delicious.

His cock twitched, hungry for more even though he was spent, was sure he wouldn't be able to handle another round for at least a few hours.

He focused on her instead, on making them even and giving her another mind-blowing release.

She was warm inside, felt as good around his fingers as she had around his cock. He groaned against her and licked her harder, flicked his tongue over her bead and teased it.

"Grey!" Her hips shot up, pressing her pert nub into his mouth as she quivered and shook, her thighs trembling on either side of his head.

He suckled her as she pulsed, pride sweeping through him as he gently brought her down, and came down with her.

He purred and lapped at her, tasting her and what he had done for her.

His female was satisfied.

She sagged against the boulder. "Oh sweet gods almighty…"

That need that had faded in her slowly built again.

He was on his back a moment later, her mouth on his, attacking him fiercely as she gripped his shoulders and worked her hips against his.

His cock twitched back to life.

He grinned against her lips and rolled with her, pinning her beneath him.

Round three it was.

CHAPTER 14

Lyra wasn't sure how she was meant to walk. She could barely tie her belt around her waist. Her hands shook badly, a quiet giggle escaping her as she struggled with the simple task. Grey rested beside her, looking as spent as she felt, a hazy edge to his blue eyes as he stared off into the distance, away from the dragon village.

"It's a good thing we can rest at the village," she said, longing for a bed.

And maybe round number four with Grey.

He was insatiable.

Although, she was hardly holding back herself.

"We're not going back."

Her fingers paused at their work and she looked at Grey. His eyes remained fixed on the distance.

"What do you mean, we're not going back?" And why did he suddenly feel nervous again? She looked back at the dragon village. "Did something happen?"

The way he refused to look at her and the sudden spike in his nerves said that something had happened, and he didn't want to talk about it.

He picked up his backpack, slung it over his shoulders and started walking in the opposite direction to the dragons.

Lyra finished with her belt and hurried after him. "What about the gem? I'm not in the habit of not paying my debts."

He growled over his shoulder at her, his blue eyes flashing fire. "You are never setting foot in that place again, do you understand?"

She stilled, wanted to growl right back at him for threatening her and thinking he could order her around, but she held it back, because she could see in his eyes, and she could feel in him, that it wasn't a male need to make her submit to him and to control her that had him laying down the law.

It was concern.

"Grey." She took a step towards him. "Tell me what happened."

He huffed, turned his back on her, and started walking again. "I don't want to talk about it."

Like he hadn't wanted to talk about why he felt he was unworthy of her.

He feared how she would react.

"I have a right to know, Grey… but more than that… I want to know. I want us to be honest with each other. Aren't things better when we're honest with each other?" She caught up with him, and the way his pupils dilated to devour the blue that started to glow in his eyes said that he was well aware that things were better when they were honest with each other.

It had led to three fantastic orgasms.

"Tell me what happened." She took hold of his right hand and gently stroked her thumb across the back of it.

He looked at their linked hands, drew down a slow deep breath and sighed. "Ren threatened me."

"Son of a fucking bitch." She turned back around, intending to return to the village and beat the crap out of the dragon, but Grey's hand tightened around hers, stopping her.

She looked back at him.

Rather than the softness she expected to find in his eyes, she found hardness. Diamond hard. Glacially cold. Anger coursed through him and into her, and his hand shook against hers. She glanced at it, and wasn't surprised to find his nails were now black claws, revealing his hellcat genes.

"He threatened you," he murmured, pure fury straining his deep voice. "If I was strong enough, I would slay that dragon for you."

She could see that he meant that. She eased back around to face him, and settled her free hand against his chest as she stepped into him. He tilted his head downwards, towards her, holding her gaze, his softening as he stared into her eyes. Her eyelids slipped to half-mast when he brushed his knuckles across her cheek.

"I don't want to pay the price he demanded for your safety, Lyra... I cannot." He averted his gaze and slowly closed his eyes. "I don't want to do that sort of thing. You'd hate me for it."

What had the dragon wanted him to do in exchange for her freedom?

He exhaled, sucked down another breath and sighed that one out too. She squeezed his hand, showing him that she was with him, and that she could never hate him.

"The Archangel team I was tracking for my brother... I think they're the ones nearby. Ren... he wanted me to capture them for him." He opened his eyes and looked into hers, his silvery eyebrows furrowing. "He wants them as replacements for the captives Archangel took from him, ones they viewed as some sort of spoil of war."

Lyra felt herself pale as that sank in. "He wants to make them all slaves."

"I didn't want to do it... I don't want to do it... but if I didn't—" He cut himself off.

She nodded. "I know. You would have done it for my sake."

To protect her.

Even though he feared she would hate him for giving those innocent people to the dragons as slaves, and would hate himself too.

"Let's get out of here." She snatched hold of his hand, threading her fingers between his, and tugged him away from the village.

The dragon could go fuck himself. She wasn't going to pay him anything in exchange for removing her shackles, not now that she knew what sort of a sick bastard he was, and knew the horrible thing he had tried to force Grey to do in order to protect her.

She started walking with Grey, as quickly as she could manage, heading along the worn path over the black mountain. The range extended southwards, towards the portal Brink had pointed out to her.

The pebbles on the path bit into her feet as she started the descent, tugging Grey along behind her. When she skidded, he caught her around her waist and pulled her up against him.

His bare chest pressed against her back, all hard muscle and heat.

She purred in response.

He was still a moment and then he purred too, the rumble echoing through the point where they pressed together and into her.

He lowered his head and swept his lips across her shoulder as he tightened his arm around her to bring her closer still, and she leaned into him, forgot what she was meant to be doing as she gave herself over to the feel of his kiss, and the tender need behind it.

She tilted her head without thinking, giving him access to her neck, and he growled against her skin and ran his tongue up the side of her throat, and teased her earlobe with his short fangs.

A tremor wracked her.

Hot and fierce.

Delicious.

She shifted her head forwards.

His warm breath skated across the nape of her neck.

His eyes drilled into it.

His heart laboured against her back and the hands that held her began to shake.

"Lyra," he uttered, a broken and strained sound, one filled with part plea and part pain.

She was pushing him too hard again, but it had proven something.

That need she had felt go through him when they had been making love, one she had thought she had imagined at the time and had put down to coming from her, it had been real.

He wanted to mark her nape.

He wanted to be her mate.

She gave him the relief he needed, lifting her hand and shifting her hair to conceal the nape of her neck.

He breathed a sigh of relief and pressed his forehead against the back of her head.

Lyra shifted to face him, but he started walking again before she could ask him the question balanced on the tip of her tongue, one that would confirm a feeling she'd had for a while now.

He clutched her hand tightly as he led her down the mountain, his eyes fixed ahead of him. She followed in silence, pulling her thoughts together and mulling over everything that had happened.

Right back to the moment they had met.

The moment that was at the very heart of the question she wanted to ask him.

When they hit the valley floor, he paused and removed his pack, and rifled through it. He offered her his canteen. She took it, glad to feel how heavy it was. Her tiger had at least had the sense to get a refill from the dragons before she had run off like some lovesick girl with a broken heart.

She swigged the water. It was still cool, so refreshing that she wanted to pour it over herself and scrub all the dirt away.

Damn, she wanted a bath.

Maybe a certain tiger could scrub her back.

He took the canteen when she offered it back to him.

"Have you ever felt there's maybe a reason you attacked the auction that day?" she said and his motions slowed, a frown marring his handsome face. "Maybe one other than what had happened to your siblings, but related to your need to protect others."

His right eyebrow arched.

She fought a bout of nerves and tried to keep them out of her voice as she spoke.

"Did you feel something that day?"

He lowered the canteen from his lips, capped it and shrugged. "Anger. Pure anger. I wanted to kill the people leading that caravan of slaves. I wanted to free them."

"And when you did?" Her question stopped him midway through putting the canteen back in his pack, freezing him like a statue.

He stared blankly at the ground for a few seconds.

And then he looked at her.

"The need abated... but then it came back. Stronger than before." His dark-silver eyebrows met in another hard frown. "It was just because I knew other slaves were nearby and I wanted to free them too."

Lyra edged closer to him, heart jittering in her throat. "What if you sensed me?"

Grey stared at her. "You were too far away. My senses—"

"The hellcat in you would be aware of me even over a greater distance than that," she cut in.

He looked as if he was having trouble believing that. "I didn't know my senses were that strong."

"They aren't... normally." She resisted the urge to fidget with the belt of her shorts and kept her eyes locked with his.

They narrowed. "What are you saying?"

Lyra moved forwards again, a single step that brought them back into contact, and pressed her palms to his chest, over his heart. It drummed hard and strong against her hands, a powerful beat that echoed in her veins.

She tilted her head back to hold his gaze, and whispered, "You know what I'm saying, Grey. I'm saying you're my fated one… and I'm yours, and that's the reason you attacked the auction."

He went still, his breath hitching as he stared into her eyes.

"You did it because you needed to find me, and protect me."

His eyes widened.

She could see it as it dawned on him, as everything fell into place.

"I felt relieved the moment I saw you… drawn to you… and unwilling to leave without you." He gathered her closer, wrapping his arms around her. His eyes leaped between hers, searching them. "You're right. I was satisfied when I freed the slaves in the caravan… but then I felt something… I became aware of something and I lost it."

Because he had needed to protect her.

His hellcat instincts had driven him, had seized control and pushed him to find her, to fight to reach her and to claim her.

"How long have you known?" His blue eyes continued to scour hers.

That trickle of fear returned, running through his veins.

"I think I knew it from the moment you walked into that tavern and I wanted to claw out the eyes of any female who so much as glanced at you."

She thought he might smile at that.

He frowned instead. "You've known that long and you didn't leave when I let you?"

She frowned right back at him. "You don't let me do anything. I do what I want."

"See… this is what I mean. You know I have hellcat blood—"

Lyra silenced him with a kiss. He fell for it for a few seconds, his mouth moving against hers, tongue teasing and tempting her to take things further.

He pushed her back and scowled at her.

She huffed at him, and then sighed when she caught the glimmer of hurt in his eyes, one that drummed in his blood too. He was thinking bad things about himself again. If she ever met his pride, she was going to show them just how vicious a hellcat could be.

She lifted her hand and rubbed her thumb across the space between his eyebrows, smoothing out the wrinkles so he would stop frowning at her.

He relented.

That was better. He was handsome when he scowled at her, but she much preferred him this way, his face soft with affection and maybe a hint of submission. Just a smidgen. She liked having this big, powerful male at her mercy, looking at her as if he would do anything for her, would be a kitten for her and her alone.

"You're nothing like a hellcat male, Grey. You're caring, protective. Wonderful." She smiled when a hint of rose spread across his cheeks. "I know you would never hurt me. You would never try to collar me."

He growled at that, gathered her in his arms and pressed his forehead against hers. "Never."

His palms brushed her neck, and she shivered as he tenderly caressed it, all of his love in that soft touch, together with the desire she could feel in him, the one that told her he would take away her scars if he could.

Lyra lifted her head and captured his lips, kissed him softly and hoped he would feel in it that desire touched her deeply, would have had her falling harder for him.

But she was already in love with him.

CHAPTER 15

"You sure you don't want my boots?" Grey looked down at Lyra's feet, at the meagre protection his socks offered her.

He had made her borrow his dirty pair too, so they formed a double layer on her feet, but it still wasn't enough to satisfy him.

"You sure you don't want to stop asking me that?" she said, the smile curving the corners of her lips at odds with the sharp bite in her tone.

He wanted to sigh.

Not one of exasperation, but one of a strange sort of happiness.

They had fallen into an easy camaraderie over the past day they had been marching south, the air between them clear at last, freeing them both from its oppressive weight. Gods, it felt good to have it all out there in the open, nothing hidden from her anymore, and to have her stay at his side.

More than that, she stole kisses whenever he let her, and had held his hand for hours.

She had even slept in his arms when they had taken shelter in a small cave at the base of one of the mountains, both of them needing rest.

Grey hadn't been able to sleep.

The novelty of holding a female while she had been sleeping, of her trusting him to protect her when she was vulnerable, had kept him awake and watching her, absorbing how good it had felt in case it never happened again.

Lyra nudged his hand with hers, knocking the backs of them together, and he looked down at her delicate little hand and then up into her eyes. They sparkled at him, tranquil tropical blue.

Called to him.

He could feel her, could feel the need as it steadily built inside her again.

The desire.

She wanted him again.

Fuck, he wanted her every second of the day.

She playfully tugged at his fingers, and he slowed to a halt and came to face her, giving in to her.

He swiftly banded his right arm around her waist, lifted her as she squeaked, and seized her lips. She moaned, her hands coming down on his bare shoulders, nails pressing in as she clutched him tightly and stroked her tongue along the seam of his lips. He opened to her, groaned as she tangled her tongue with his and teased his fangs, sending a shiver down his spine.

Sweet fucking gods, he would never get enough of this.

He would never get enough of her.

Her legs wrapped around his waist and he groaned again, this one strained as he cupped her backside and held her against him. Her shorts were loose enough that he could feel all of her natural curves beneath his fingers, together with her heat as it pressed against his stomach just above the waist of his trousers.

He slowly lowered her, needing to feel that heat somewhere else.

Somewhere that ached for her.

"Grey," she murmured against his lips as he settled her against his already rock hard length.

He turned with her, broke away from her lips and scoured the desolate valley for a place where he could take her, somewhere they might have at least a little privacy.

She tensed.

His senses went on high alert and he swiftly looked up at her to check her. She stared off into the distance over his shoulder in the direction they had been heading.

He looked there too.

"What's that?" She pointed, and he tracked her finger, following it to find what she had spotted.

Something was there in the gloom.

A long way away.

He squinted, focused harder and let his animal side rise to the fore a little, enough that his vision sharpened and the world around him brightened, and he could see what she had.

Lights.

They were steady. Bright. White.

These weren't flaming torches.

They were manmade.

"You think it's the ones you're looking for?" Lyra whispered, as if they would be able to hear her from such a distance.

Still, it paid to be cautious.

His senses didn't reveal anyone in the area other than him and Lyra, but he wasn't going to risk it.

"It's possible," he said in a low voice and lowered her to her feet. He looked back in the direction they had come, and then in the one they had been heading. They had been following the mountain range from the dragon village, and the Devil's domain had been to their left the entire time, meaning they had certainly been heading in the right direction to cross paths with the mortals. "The dragons said they were a day's march south-east, and that's the course we've been taking to reach the portal."

"We should check it out."

He whipped around to face her. "No."

He wasn't taking her anywhere near Archangel. If they saw her and realised what she was, well it didn't bear thinking about. Talon had gone through hell at their hands and he was just a tiger, a common enough species of shifter. Archangel would go to town on a hellcat.

Grey wanted to get her to the portal as soon as possible.

He wanted to get her home, where she would be safe.

She sidled closer to him, the feel of her near to him comforting him and soothing his fear of something happening to her.

He glanced down at her, and his gaze caught on hers, on the worry that shone in it.

"I don't want you coming back to Hell, Grey," she whispered, her dark eyebrows furrowing. "I know you will if you don't find out what the humans are doing. You need to help your brother, and that need will bring you back to this realm."

He sighed, brushed the knuckles of his right hand across her cheek, and wanted to deny that to alleviate her worry, but he couldn't lie to her.

Her concern touched him, warmed his heart in a way he had never experienced before. He didn't want her worrying about him, and he certainly didn't want her demanding to come with him when he returned to Hell, so there was only one course of action open to him.

"Fine. We'll take a look as we're passing."

Just a peek.

Although he knew it wouldn't be enough to assuage his own curiosity about what Archangel were doing in Hell. That curiosity had only grown since meeting the dragons and hearing that the squad he was looking for weren't the only ones in Hell. There were others, and they were forcing fae to work the portals so they could come and go as they pleased.

He kept his eyes locked on the lights in the distance to his left as they started walking again.

He already wanted a closer look, and once he had that, he was going to want to rattle a few answers loose from one of the hunters, and maybe give them a little payback for what they had done to his pride, attacking it for no reason.

He led Lyra up a path that looked as if it ran along the base of the mountain around twenty feet up from the valley floor. A good vantage point. He ushered her in front of him as the path narrowed, torn between having her take the lead where she would be vulnerable to any hunter that might be ahead of them, and having her bring up the rear where he couldn't see her.

He needed to see her, needed eyes on her at all times.

She reached behind her, and he looked down at the hand she offered. He slipped his into it and clutched it tightly as he silently thanked her for picking up on his fear and his need to know she was safe and for helping him soothe them both.

When they were in line with the hunter camp, Lyra stepped off the path and skidded silently down the slope. He followed her and ended up next to her behind a large boulder. She peered around it.

Grey huffed.

The hunters were on the other side of the valley, too far away for him to see what they were doing.

He wanted to get a head count before he did anything, needed to know how many hunters he would be dealing with if he approached the camp and tried to get some answers about that damned door.

He turned to Lyra to say they should sneak closer for a better look.

The scent of blood hit him.

Shrieks and terrified screams shattered the silence.

Grey snapped his head towards the hunter camp, the odour of blood growing thicker in the hot air as he tried to see what was happening.

Who the fuck was killing all the mortals he had intended to interrogate?

He could feel his chance slipping through his fingers as he studied the darkness ahead of him, searching it for a sign of what was attacking the mortals.

Lyra leaped the rock and started sprinting towards the battle, keeping as low to the ground as possible to avoid detection.

He growled and gave chase, his heart slamming against his ribs as his need to protect her screamed that she was going to hurl herself into the fray blind, with no plan and no clue as to what was happening.

The remaining sensible part of him tried to rise above it and hammer home that she was only trying to get a closer look. He knew that. She was moving low, silent in the darkness. She wasn't launching an assault.

But his instinct to protect her was too strong, overruled sense and roared that she was going to fight and get herself hurt. Or worse.

That had his stomach churning, heart racing and limbs trembling as he sprinted after her, scanning the distance ahead of her as the battle drew closer.

What the hell was happening ahead of him?

Had the mortals strayed too close to a dragon's territory and were paying the price?

He searched the dull golden sky.

Surely a dragon would choose to decimate the mortals in its beast form though?

The skies were clear.

Lyra ground to a halt around sixty metres from the battle.

Her fear flooded him.

Everything slowed as she turned towards him, her long black hair splaying outwards and her blue eyes going impossibly wide.

"Run!"

Had she spotted the dragon he couldn't see?

He ignored her and ran towards her instead, reached his right arm out to her and willed her to run to him, his every instinct screaming at him to protect her.

A burst of air battered him, a blast of black dust sweeping over him as the ground bucked and shook, and he quickly covered his face with his arms to protect his vision from the particles.

What was out there?

Unsettling silence fell.

He lowered his hands from his face as the air cleared around him.

Something drove hard into his gut, lifted his boots from the ground and sent him flying high into the air.

The world zoomed away from him, pain arcing like lightning through his body, zinging along his bones. He growled and ripped his backpack off, gripped one of the straps between his teeth and shifted the moment the pain dulled enough to allow him to transform.

He twisted and turned in the air as he came down, eyes darting as he swiftly charted the distance between him and the ground.

This was going to hurt like a bitch.

He flipped one last time and landed hard on all four paws, his bones taking the brunt of the impact, sending another blast of pain shooting through him, one that came close to forcing him to shift back into his human form.

Thank fuck for feline bone structure and its ability to absorb impacts.

He wasn't sure he had ever been so grateful for it.

He dropped his pack and kicked out of his clothes, freeing himself so he could fight.

Grey lifted his head and snarled at the one who had tossed him as he prowled forwards.

The male stared him down, towering close to seven feet tall, his powerful body encased in heavy black armour that mimicked the muscles beneath. A horned helmet flared from back from above his nose and wisps of long golden hair danced from beneath it, not fitting with his dark appearance.

The crimson eyes that narrowed on Grey matched it perfectly though.

Together with the undeniable aura of pure evil that hovered around the male.

And his huge black feathered wings.

Not a dragon.

A fucking angel.

A fallen one at that.

He had come for Lyra.

CHAPTER 16

The fallen angel slowly turned to face Lyra. She stood her ground, refusing to reveal her fear to him. Black mist writhed over his obsidian armour as he moved, caressing it like a lover, and trailed from the long black claws of his gauntlets.

His smile gained a cold edge. "You were difficult to find. I was beginning to think I would have to kill every slave I placed a tracker on before I found you."

He frowned as he looked at her wrists, his displeasure on seeing her shackles gone written in every line of his sculpted face.

Behind him, Grey edged towards her, his white markings bright in the dim light. He circled the male and she did her best to keep the angel's eyes on her, giving him time to close ranks with her.

The fallen angel's crimson gaze slid towards his right, towards Grey, and narrowed, a glow illuminating his elliptical pupils.

"It would be wise of you not to interfere," he drawled, his deep voice barren of feeling. "I am feeling a little testy after losing one hellcat and I will not be held responsible for how badly it will end for you if you stand in my way."

Grey bared his fangs in response to that, his blue eyes bright and pupils wide as he hunted the male. He slinked towards her, his head held low and his gaze never leaving the fallen angel. His long banded tail twitched, the only outward sign of his nerves.

Fear that she could feel in him.

Fear that pounded through her too.

The fallen angel stared Grey down and then his scarlet eyes flicked to her, sending a shiver through her as a sickening sensation swept over her, a darkness that seemed to drain the light from her soul.

"I will get enough gold from your sale to set me up for at least another century."

This time, she bared her fangs at him. Like hell. She wasn't going to let him take her into captivity and sell her. She would die before that happened, and she would die a free hellcat.

The fallen angel slid his gaze back to Grey. "I can cut you in on the deal. Just step aside and you can have ten percent of the coin I will make on her. Think of it as a finder's fee."

Lyra's heart kicked hard.

Grey soothed it by baring his fangs on a hiss, his ears flattening as they flared backwards.

And then he launched at the male.

They clashed hard, but Grey was no match for the fallen angel. The male easily shook him before he could strike with his fangs, sending him sprawling across the black ground. Grey rolled onto his feet and attacked again, his claws not strong enough to break through the male's heavy armour as he raked them down his leg.

The fallen angel kicked him in the gut, lifting his paws from the earth, and Grey hissed and whimpered.

Lyra snarled, stripped off her clothes and shifted, her bones aching as they grew and shrank, morphed into a new shape, and black fur sweeping over her skin. She hit the earth running as her twin tails whipped out from the base of her spine and blue flames erupted down their lengths and beneath her paws.

The fallen angel looked her way.

She roared and kicked off, leaped high into the air and sailed towards him.

Rather than smacking her away as he had with Grey, the male tried to catch her. *Shit*. She twisted in the air, realising her mistake, and pressed her back paws hard into his chest. She kicked with all of her strength, springing free of his reach and knocking him backwards before he could capture her. She landed on the ground and the male grunted.

Her head snapped around.

Grey scrambled on the male's back, claws raking over his shoulders, seeking purchase. He snarled and sank his fangs into the fallen angel's black feathered wings, ripping a cry from the male's lips.

Inside, she grinned, a flicker of pride warming her heart.

That was her warrior.

He had found a weak spot.

The fallen angel reached over his head, grabbed Grey by the scruff of his neck, and tossed him. He hit the dirt a few metres beyond Lyra, his pain echoing through her, and refused to remain down. He lumbered onto his feet and she took a step towards him as he shook his head and she saw the crimson staining the back of his neck.

The angel had sunk claws into Grey.

The scent of his blood hit her hard, ripped a cry from her throat and had her flames burning hotter, sweeping up her legs and spreading over her hind quarters.

Fire blazed through her veins like an inferno too, pushing her to act, and she couldn't deny it or the need to sink her fangs into the fallen angel and rip him to shreds.

The bastard would pay for hurting her male.

She leaped at the fallen angel, her roar echoing around the mountains and sending the blue fire fluttering outwards from her teeth.

He raised his left arm to block her and she wrapped her jaws around it, hung on for dear life and bit down. His armour was solid, making her fangs ache, but she forced herself to bite harder, using all of her strength on the bastard.

The metal gave beneath the pressure.

Grey came out of nowhere, a ghost in the low light, and hit the male's left wing hard, gripping it in his claws and fangs, dragging the male off balance. The fallen angel ripped her off him, but didn't throw her aside. He dropped her at his feet and turned, reaching for Grey.

It struck her that he didn't want to hurt her.

He didn't want to damage the goods.

As he twisted to reach Grey, he left his back exposed to her.

Lyra growled and leaped on it just as he dislodged Grey and sent him tumbling hard and fast across the black dirt. His pain echoed through her, driving her on. She struck hard, sinking fangs into the angel's right wing and tearing at it.

"Fucking pest," the male snarled and grabbed her, the sensation of darkness and danger he emanated rising, sparking a desire to run as far as she could from him.

It was hard to ignore that instinct and to keep fighting him as he hauled her in front of him and held her there by the scruff of her neck as if she weighed nothing.

Grey growled from behind her.

The male tossed him a smirk, one that spoke of victory and flashed fangs.

A sickening cold swept through her.

She had let herself get caught.

He beat his wings.

She struggled like a wild thing, clawing and kicking at him, catching his face and neck and leaving long red marks on his pale skin. No. She couldn't let him fly away with her.

He had barely lifted off the earth when Grey landed on his back, savaging his left wing, sending feathers flying everywhere. The male howled and grabbed him, swinging her with him as he twisted at the waist, and she struggled again as he threw Grey, harder this time.

She winced as he hit the dirt, rolled and shifted back into his human form. Grey.

She kicked hard and fast at the fallen angel's face with her back paws, a need to escape and check on Grey fuelling her.

The fallen angel glared at her, and beat his wings. His face screwed up, pain flashed in his crimson eyes, and he growled through long fangs as he looked at his left wing.

Relief crashed over her.

It was broken.

Grey's last attack had torn a long gash down the curve of his black wing, exposing tendons and shredding muscle.

He couldn't fly away with her.

She looked back at Grey.

Her heart stopped in her chest.

He was running away from her, into the distance.

The fallen angel laughed mirthlessly. "You need to get yourself a better male than that one."

She looked back at him and growled, could read between the lines to see that he was insinuating that she should choose a male like him over Grey.

Never.

She bared her fangs, her fury rising, and her flames rose with it, coursed over her body and licked at her black fur.

When they reached her neck, the fallen angel hissed and released her, and stared at his hand.

The black metal of his gauntlet glowed red hot.

He growled and shot his other hand out towards her, long claws slicing through the air.

Something silver swept across them.

The fallen angel staggered backwards, his agonised bellow echoing around the valley and ringing in her ears.

She stared, blinked, unsure what had happened.

Until she saw the two fingers on the dirt in front of her, and Grey rushed past her, two silver blades clutched tightly in his fists as he thundered towards the fallen angel and attacked him, driving the male away from her.

Gods.

He was glorious as he fought, his expression savage as his eyes glowed bright blue. His muscles shifted beneath his bare skin with his fluid and graceful movements, his twin swords slicing grooves in the fallen angel's black armour, cutting deeper with each strike.

For every blow the angel managed to block, Grey landed one with his other sword. He didn't give the male space, kept pushing forwards, taking whatever strikes the male landed on his flesh, weathering them as he battered the male, attempting to overpower him.

Lyra growled and rushed towards him.

The fallen angel finally gained some space, using his battered wings to carry him a few metres backwards through the air. Grey gave chase, lowering both of his blades to his side as he sprinted towards the male.

The shadows that writhed around the fallen angel swept downwards to his right hand and gathered there, forming a shape.

Her eyes widened.

The fallen angel grinned.

Grey skidded into a hard right turn when the shadows formed a huge black blade in the fallen angel's hand and he swung it, slicing through the air where Grey had been a second before. Grey snarled and zigzagged, kicking dust up as he evaded each strike of the male's broadsword.

She growled and sprang at the fallen angel as he gave her his back. He snarled and battered her with his one good wing, making it impossible to keep hold of him. She landed at his feet and he turned on her, raising his sword at the same time.

Grey roared and she gasped as he appeared behind the male, sailing through the air, both of his blades held downwards and directed at the male's back.

The fallen angel turned on a pinhead and brought his black sword up, sweeping it in a fierce diagonal arc towards Grey.

She growled and leaped at his left arm, sinking fangs into his armour and pulling it back with her weight as she dropped to the ground.

Throwing his blow off course.

Grey struck hard, driving one of his blades into the fallen angel's shoulder as the male twisted with her. The fallen angel grunted and jammed his arm into her mouth with so much force her teeth ached and she lost her grip on him. He moved faster than she could track, his injured left hand flying towards Grey.

Who growled and tried to evade, leaning hard to his left. The male's fist slammed into his face and Grey grunted as he fell, leaving one of his blades lodged in the angel's shoulder.

The fallen angel snarled as he pulled it free and blood sprayed from the wound, quickly falling to a trickle that chased down the black plates of his chest armour. He tossed the blade aside and advanced on Grey, the black mist that writhed around him growing agitated and that oily sensation of darkness growing thicker, pressing down on her.

She pushed onto her paws.

Grey readied his one remaining blade, but he was unsteady on his feet, the deep lacerations across his chest, stomach and thighs taking their toll on him as they dripped crimson.

She couldn't let him fight alone.

She focused on her flames and stoked them hotter, so they warmed her fur and covered all of her.

The male thrust towards Grey with his broadsword. Grey leaped backwards, dodging the blow, but the angel smiled coldly, as if he had landed it, as if he knew victory would be his now.

He threw his injured left hand towards Grey.

Grey instinctively blocked, even though the male held nothing in it.

And then he was shooting towards the angel as the male curled his injured hand towards him.

Powerless to stop himself.

She snarled as the angel pulled him through the air using telekinesis.

Roared as the bastard's black sword pierced Grey's left side and her male cried out.

Blood poured down his hip and his leg, stark crimson that had her vision turning blue as her fury overwhelmed her and her instincts seized command, driving her to protect her male.

Her mate.

The fallen angel pressed a boot to Grey's hip and shoved him off the blade, tearing another pained bellow from Grey's lips. He staggered backwards, fought to remain standing and dropped to one knee.

The male turned glowing red eyes on her.

His power swept over her, pressed down on her, had one thought spinning through her mind as she charged.

They weren't going to win this.

Resignation rushed through her.

A huge black paw shot out of the gloom, landed on the fallen angel's back and slammed him face-first into the dirt.

Her eyes shot wide.

Brink.

The enormous black dragon threw his head back, his long horns almost touching his wings as he spread them, and roared.

The fallen angel screamed as Brink used his talons to rip away the back plate of his armour and tear through his feathered wings, and hastily pushed backwards, under the paw that held him as Brink's head came down.

His huge fangs snapped together, narrowly missing the fallen angel's head.

The dragon grunted and lifted his paw, revealing the fallen angel as he staggered onto his feet. He drove his blade into Brink's paw again, forcing him to back away.

Grey found his feet and ran at the fallen angel, his pain beating in her veins with each step. She growled and joined him, raced alongside him as they closed the distance between them and the angel.

The male swung their way, bringing his black sword around and holding it at an angle in front of him, blocking Grey's blow as her male struck hard with his silver blade.

Brink snarled and raked a talon down the angel's back, caught it in the back of his armoured trousers, and slammed him back into the dirt.

When the dragon lifted the male again, Grey was there, thrusting his sword forwards.

The fallen angel didn't have a chance to block.

The silver blade pierced his chest, sank hilt-deep into it and punched out of his back.

The male threw his head back and unleashed an unholy scream that sent a chill sweeping through her and had every hair on her sleek body rising.

Brink's left wing came down, knocking her and Grey backwards, sending them both sprawling across the ground.

She found her paws again and looked back at Brink.

Crimson light burst from behind his wing, visible through the leathery black membrane, and shone across his chest. He reared back, closing his eyes and tilting his head away.

The ground trembled and then bucked, and she sank low to it, dug her claws in as it shook beneath her, and the red light grew so bright it hurt her eyes.

She closed them just as a shockwave swept across the land from the direction of Brink, battering her and knocking her backwards, sending her tumbling further away from the dragon.

Wet slapping sounds filled the silence in the aftermath of the explosion.

The heavy scent of blood made her gag.

She cracked her eyes open and grimaced at the sight of Brink.

His wing and his body had shielded her and Grey from most of the blood and gore, pieces of flesh and bone sticking to his black scales and rolling down his leathery wing.

She gagged again.

Brink sneered, flashing a lot of fangs as he looked himself over, and then he reared back, turned away from her and beat his wings. For a moment, she thought he was leaving.

Pieces of the fallen angel hit the ground hard, thrown from his body by the powerful action of beating his wings.

"Are you okay?" Grey said from behind her.

Lyra shifted into her mortal form and looked back at him, an answer balanced on her lips, a reassurance that she was fine.

He collapsed, landing on his face in the black dirt.

"Grey!" Lyra rushed to him and skidded to her knees beside him.

She pulled him over, grunting at his dead weight, and her eyes widened. There was so much blood. Tears lined her eyes as she stared at the wound on his side, a deep hole that spilled crimson in thick rivulets. Her hands shook as she reached out to touch it, heart aching as she pressed her palms to it and tried to stem the bleeding, her hands slipping around in the warm liquid.

Gods, she was free, but at what cost?

She was going to lose the only male she had ever loved.

She was going to lose her mate.

Brink stopped beside her, back in his human form and clad in his black leather trousers, wearing a concerned look on his rough face as he studied Grey. He crouched on the other side of him to her, lifted his eyes from him and gave her back a spark of hope, one that she clung to as fiercely as she clung to Grey.

"Hold him, and keep him as still as you can," he whispered.

He ran his midnight eyes over Grey again and shimmering sparks of violet and gold emerged from their depths.

The tinny scent of magic joined the odour of Grey's blood in the air.

A shiver chased over her skin and she gripped Grey's shoulder with one hand and his leg with the other, and pressed him into the dirt with all the strength she could muster.

Brink nodded in approval. "Just… hold on… no matter what… hold him down."

Lyra didn't have a clue what he was going to do, but she nodded to let him know she would do her best, and that she trusted him.

Grey's life was in his hands now.

Brink placed his palms on Grey's stomach on either side of the wound and stared at it, his eyes brightening, that scent of magic growing stronger, swirling around her and making the hairs on her arms stand on end.

The dragon smiled faintly at Grey.

"This is going to hurt you a lot less than it's going to hurt me."

CHAPTER 17

Darkness surrounded him.

The pained roar that echoed around it resonated within him too, but he wasn't sure it had come from his soul. Fierce and fiery agony blazed in every inch of him, rolled to new heights that seemed to rip pieces of him away, and this time he was sure the roar that rumbled through the inky black like thunder had issued from his lips.

Had been dragged from the pit of his weary soul.

The flames scorched his bones. Seared his flesh.

Felt as if they would burn all of him away and leave nothing.

In the wake of the fire, came light.

It rolled through the darkness, a beam that cut through the endless black and drew him to it.

As the pain began to fade, a voice reached his ears.

Calling to him.

Speaking his name.

Lyra.

He strained towards that voice, reached for it and pushed forwards, determined to shake the midnight tendrils that tried to pull him back, that snagged his legs and wrapped around his arms.

He was coming.

He could feel her fear, her pain, and he was coming to take it all away.

The inky vines holding his legs and arms snapped as the beam of light reached him and he sank into it.

His eyes fluttered open, revealing more darkness.

And then that ray of light.

Lyra.

She leaned over him, tears wobbling on her long black lashes and her blue eyes overflowing with happiness he could feel in her.

"What happened?" he croaked, and grimaced at how tight his throat was, and the ache that reached right down to his marrow and filled every molecule of his body.

"Brink helped us… he brought you back." She tried to smile, and tears skated down her cheeks, cutting through the ash and the blood.

Gods. His beautiful Lyra. He had been sure that it had been the end for him, and rather than being calm and taking comfort from the thought of running with his ancestors, he had been filled with cold and fear, with terror that he had known would live on forever inside him.

All because he had thought he would never see her again.

Because he couldn't bear the thought of being parted from her.

His beautiful mate.

The first and only female he would ever love.

She clutched his hand above his stomach and brought it to her chest, pressed it there and held it so tightly that he knew she felt the same way about him, that the thought of being parted from him had been destroying her.

He wanted to drown in her, to stare at her forever and never stop looking at her, but he owed a dragon a great debt, one he felt sure he would never be able to repay.

He tilted his head right, towards Brink.

The black-haired warrior sat on his haunches, breathing hard, his skin ashen and slick with sweat. Exhaustion echoed in his dull obsidian eyes as they remained locked on him, firmly away from Lyra.

Grey was thankful for that too.

He was too tired to lose his shit over the male looking at her when she was naked.

"Thank you," he whispered, but knew as he looked at Brink that simple thank you wasn't enough.

The male looked close to passing out, and he knew that first bellow of agony, one that had sounded as if its owner was ripping their own soul apart, losing a piece of themselves in the process, had come from Brink.

Whatever magic he had used to heal Grey's wounds and give him another chance at life, it had cost him greatly.

Brink nodded.

Sagged a little and landed on his arse on the black dirt.

He sat there, his forearms resting on his bent knees, breathing hard.

"What happened?" Brink panted and pulled down one long breath and tried to exhale it slowly.

It didn't happen. It ended up sharp and short, followed by another deep fast breath. He gritted his teeth, a muscle in his jaw popping, and grunted as he ran trembling hands over his wild black hair and muttered something to himself.

Grey mustered the strength to speak.

"We think they were the Archangel team mentioned in Grey's documents, the ones carrying out the research for the project his brother was interested in finding out more about." Lyra beat him to it, and he looked at her, soul-deep grateful for her stepping up and sparing him so he could conserve the tattered remains of his strength.

"The fallen angel?" Brink curled a lip at the blood staining his bare arms and chest.

"Was after me," Lyra said. "I'm sorry about that."

The dragon casually shrugged. "A dead fallen angel is a good fallen angel. They're a menace."

"What were you doing here?" Grey pushed the words out as he felt a little stronger, the pain dulling to a manageable level where he could breathe easier and didn't feel as if his bones were crumbling beneath his skin.

He flexed his fingers, testing their strength as it slowly returned.

Brink seemed more relaxed too, his breathing level at last. "Ren sent me when you disappeared. He doesn't like people reneging on a contract."

"I wasn't," she snapped. "I always pay my debts. I was going to get the gem."

"I wasn't talking about you." Brink's black eyes fell to Grey as he pushed himself up into a sitting position. "Still… I suppose you are off the hook now… and I didn't exactly agree with what Ren wanted you to do."

It was a relief to hear that.

Brink stared off to his left, towards the dead hunters and the lights. "No one should be enslaved, trapped against their will."

Grey had never really thought about how the dragons felt about their banishment, but the yearning in Brink's dark eyes said it was hell for them, that they felt trapped in this bleak realm and longed for blue skies to fly in and the feel of sunshine on their scales.

"Do you know of any reason why mortals are interested in this place?" He gripped Lyra's shoulder and tried to stand. She held his arm and helped him, rising to her feet but moving behind him as she steadied him on his.

Using him as a shield so Brink didn't see her bare curves.

Brink's gaze slid to meet his, his black eyebrows dipped low, and then his focus drifted back towards the hunters, and lifted up, to the mountains.

Grey followed his distant gaze and spotted an opening halfway up the cragged black mountain. The dim glow coming from it said the mortals had placed lights inside it too, and as he peered closer, he could just about make out ropes dangling from a ledge at the mouth of the cave.

"Why would mortals come here?" Brink stared at the cave, his voice as distant as his gaze, and Grey had the feeling that the male knew this place.

"I don't know." Grey couldn't take his eyes off it, felt drawn towards it as he stared at it, pulled there by invisible vines that snared him tightly and wouldn't release him. "I need to know."

Before he could look at Brink, could utter the question balanced on his lips, the male had shifted into an enormous black dragon and had scooped him and Lyra up into one huge paw. Lyra squeaked and pressed against him, one arm banding around his waist from behind and her other one gripping the sharp talon that curled around Grey's chest.

Grey battled the urge that blasted through him as her bare curves pressed against his and it hit him that Brink was touching her too.

Had his damned paw on Grey's naked female.

He growled but held back the need to shift and attack the male, breathed through it and focused on Lyra behind him, how she held him with both hands now, and had pressed her cheek against his shoulder. Soothing him.

The world dropped away, making his stomach lurch, and he closed his eyes and narrowed everything down to Lyra.

She was warm and soft against him, her feelings flowing into him, filled with affection, relief and tenderness that curled around him and had him sinking against her, wanting to turn and nuzzle her cheek as he held her.

Just as he was about to give in to that need, Brink's paw opened and his feet hit solid ground again. His legs wobbled but he locked his knees to stop them from giving out beneath him, and remained standing. He turned and gathered Lyra into his arms to shield her from view as Brink shifted back into his human form. Black leathers moulded over his long legs as he strode past Grey, heading into the cave.

It reeked of blood.

Grey turned his head to track the male.

His eyes slowly widened.

It was a slaughterhouse.

Crimson splashed up the rugged black walls, still glistening and wet, catching the lights.

Dead mortals lay everywhere, ripped to shreds. Some of them wore the white coats of scientists, while the rest were dressed in black fatigues.

A few lucky souls near the cave entrance had been given a swift death, only their throats cut by the fallen angel's claws.

Grey stooped beside a female hunter and removed her boots and her black combat trousers.

He offered them to Lyra where she stood closed to him, wide blue eyes scanning the horrific scene. He had no love for the mortals, probably would have killed them himself if the fallen angel hadn't. She looked as if she felt bad for them though.

It dawned on him.

"You didn't do this," he muttered and rose to his feet, and offered her the clothes again.

She started, eyes leaping to his, and quickly took the trousers and boots and put them on.

Her movement slowed as she fastened her trousers.

"He was here because of me." She looked down at her boots, and then moved past him and stripped the t-shirt from the dead female. She paused there, holding it in her hands, her eyes on the hunter.

"Don't feel sorry for these people, Lyra. They don't deserve it," Grey bit out, and when she looked at him, her soft eyes imploring him to tell her the reason he despised them, he added, "They held my brother for months, tortured him and ran tests on him, and they killed a friend of his. Their experiments broke her. And then they attacked our pride. They slaughtered innocent females and cubs… ones who couldn't defend themselves."

The guilt that had been in her blue eyes faded away, sparks of cerulean brightening her irises as anger swept in to replace it.

"They want to hurt us, Lyra. If they ever got their hands on you…" He looked away from her. "I'll *never* let it happen. They could send a thousand hunters and I wouldn't let them near you. I'd kill every single one of them."

She slipped into the t-shirt, rose onto her feet and took hold of his hand, pressing her fingers against his palm.

He looked down into her blue eyes.

Drowned in them.

"You'd do that for me?" she whispered, a shimmer to her eyes that spoke of affection and told him she had liked his fierce words.

"I meant every one of them," he murmured and stroked her cheek as he held her gaze and let her see that in his. "I swore I would protect you and I will."

She smiled, tiptoed and kissed him.

It was too brief.

She stole her lips from his just as he was getting into it, and broke free of his grip, slipping away from him, heading deeper into the cave. She whirled to face him.

"Come on. I need to know what they were doing here."

Grey smiled at that and the fact he wasn't the only cat curious about what Archangel had been up to in the dragon realm.

He grabbed a pair of trousers from a male hunter, tugged them on and buttoned them as he walked, slowly following her towards the back of the cave, giving his legs time to grow stronger. Damned if he was going to rush and end up flat on his face because of it.

He had worried Lyra enough for a lifetime.

She waited for him at the point where the open cave became a tunnel, her blue eyes fixed on him, affection brightening them and luring him towards her.

Gods.

He had never imagined a female like Lyra could be his, but as he looked at her waiting for him, her hand rising to reach for him, he knew that she was.

And she would be forever.

He held his hand out to her when he was close enough, savoured the soft warmth of her fingers as they slid over his, and how good it felt as he curled his fingers between hers and locked their hands together.

He would never let her go.

Never.

He led her into the tunnel, keeping her tucked close behind him. Lights formed a trail that took them down into the mountain. The path branched as the air began to grow warmer, splitting into three. He kept following the lights. The corridor was tight in places, the rocks closing in and making him turn sideways to squeeze through, but then it opened out.

Into an enormous cavern.

Brink stood in the centre of it, transfixed by the wall in front of him.

On it, was a detailed carving at least four metres wide by three metres in height. It must have taken someone years to carefully chip the figures into the black stone.

A dragon on the right and a female in human form on the left.

She stood on the precipice of a mountain, valleys stretching beyond her. The sun rose above a lake in the distance, its rays filling the sky, telling Grey that the scene depicted somewhere in the mortal world.

The female's long robes flowed behind her together with her wavy hair as she held her hand out to the dragon looming above her. It stood with its huge wings spread and one paw lifted from the rock, almost as if it was reaching for her too.

"Brink." Grey walked into the cavern and the male turned.

His step faltered.

Tears lined Brink's dark eyes.

"Do you know this place?" Because Grey was starting to get the impression that he did and that this place meant something to Brink.

It was important to him.

He looked beyond the male to the dragon. It looked like Brink, but then most dragons looked the same to him.

Symbols ran beneath the relief and twined around the dragon and the female.

On the black sandy floor of the cavern, drawing pads had been discarded, probably tossed aside in the panicked rush when the fallen angel had attacked. One had a sketch of the female, and the other three had drawings of the symbols, and notes scrawled around them.

Archangel didn't understand them.

Did Brink?

He lifted his gaze to the male. Brink stared at the carving again, a distant look in his dark eyes.

"It was my home once," he murmured, eyes not leaving the female on the wall. "I don't come here much now, but it was my place of hibernation a long time ago…"

"Why don't you come here?" Lyra's soft voice filled the cavern and she took a step towards Brink.

Grey could feel her curiosity. It beat inside him as fiercely as his own. Brink was the key to this place, and to understanding what was on the other side of the door in Archangel.

He knew it, felt it deep inside him.

"Something about it hurts," Brink whispered and tore his eyes away from the female, casting Grey a pained look as his eyebrows furrowed and unease settled across his features. "It dredges up feelings I don't understand… so I started staying away."

The dragon drifted towards the wall and sank to his knees by the female.

Had Brink known this female once? Had the passing of time made his mind forget her, but not his heart?

The dragon looked as if he had loved and lost, and still suffered because of it.

"What do they mean?" he said as Brink ghosted an unsteady hand over the symbols that flowed beneath the female, intricate swirls and spots, dashes and sharp angles.

They were more than decorative.

It was a language.

"I don't remember now." Brink touched one of the symbols, rested his fingers on it and stared at it. One directly beneath the female's bare feet. "I never remember. I know them, but I cannot read them. I made them, but I forgot them. They are foreign to me, but also familiar. I cannot explain it. Whenever I try to remember… I forget."

Grey moved to stand beside him so he could get a closer look at the carving. He needed answers, but he had the feeling he wasn't going to get them from Brink.

There had to be a reason Archangel had been interested in this place, in the symbols on this wall.

Brink stared blankly at the carving, his black eyes glassy, and whispered, "She always makes me forget."

Grey stilled, afraid that even the slightest movement might shake Brink out of whatever had seized him, just as it had back at the dragon village and Brink hadn't been able to remember what had happened to him.

She always made him forget.

"Who?" Grey said softly, his heart pounding, a feeling that he was close to uncovering what Archangel were doing rushing through him.

Brink murmured, "Aryanna."

Shock swept through Grey, almost knocking him on his arse.

Aryanna was the name of the project related to the door in Archangel, the one he was researching.

He hadn't thought of it as a name before now.

"Who's Aryanna, Brink." He reached out to touch Brink's shoulder.

The male blinked, his head snapped around and he stared at Grey. "Who?"

"Fuck," he growled and cursed himself.

Stupid fucking idiot.

He should have kept still, but the need to rattle more answers out of Brink had consumed him, had made him move before he could stop himself.

He crouched in front of Brink, glanced at Lyra to check she was alright, and caught the flicker of disappointment in her eyes that told her she was right there with him, was as desperate to know more about the female and was equally as frustrated that he had fucked up the chance he had been given.

"Aryanna." Grey pointed to the female on the wall and Brink's gaze followed his arm. "Remember Aryanna."

Brink stared blankly at the female. "I don't know that name."

Shit.

He was starting to get the impression that more than time was involved in Brink's little lapses in memory. Aryanna had done something to him, had somehow made him forget.

His eyes widened.

"She was a witch."

The moment Grey said that, Brink's eyes went glassy again.

"She cursed me." Brink stared at the female, tears rising in his eyes, and reached a trembling hand out to her, his eyebrows furrowing and pain washing across his features. "She cursed us all."

A shiver went through Grey.

Brink slowly slid his gaze towards him.

"She banished us to Hell."

"Fucking hell," Grey breathed and sank onto his backside as that hit him.

Archangel had to want the spell she had used, one that was powerful enough to banish a species and stop them from entering the mortal realm by stripping them of their powers and inflicting a slow death upon them if they dared to set foot in it.

He stared at the carving of the female, and the cold that had been sweeping through him turned to ice.

It was more than that.

He had read the Project Aryanna file a thousand times over, looking for clues, enough times that he could recite most of it by heart.

In one of the related files, it had mentioned a subject and something about a barrier, and power they needed to break it.

He had thought nothing of it at the time, had figured it was just another poor soul being held in one of the cages as his brother had been.

But why would Archangel want to break a barrier around one of their own detainees?

"What happened to Aryanna, Brink?" He pointed to the female. "Archangel mentioned holding a subject, and something about breaking a barrier. Is it possible the file was talking about her?"

How long did witches live? The dragons had been banished millennia ago. Was it possible a witch could live that long?

Brink stared at her, pain flooding his eyes, and reached for her, stroked his fingers down her figure and growled, "She is linked to me… and I to her… what she took from me… I gave to her… what I took from her… she gave to me."

That didn't make any sense.

He grabbed Brink's shoulder.

The male turned on him with a snarl and batted his hand away. "She is *mine*."

Before Grey could stop him, Brink was gone, out of the cavern.

He chased after him, leaving Lyra to follow, and reached the entrance to the main cave just as Brink hit the ledge and ground to a halt there. The wind whipped his wild black hair around his face as he turned towards Grey and his eyes glowed violet and gold.

"She will be mine again."

Brink dropped off the ledge, disappearing from view, and Grey sprinted towards it, hitting the edge just as a huge black dragon shot past the mouth of the cave.

Heading south.

"You don't think he's…" Lyra stopped beside him, her eyes tracking Brink.

Grey nodded. "He's going to get himself killed though."

"Then he's going to need our help." Lyra placed her hand into his.

He looked down at her and shook his head as he saw the need to fight in her bright blue eyes, a need that echoed in him.

He knew the answer to what was beyond the door now, meaning his mission was over, but it wasn't going to be enough to satisfy Talon's curiosity.

Because it wasn't enough to satisfy his own.

The need to know what Archangel wanted with Aryanna had only grown now that he knew she was the one responsible for cursing an entire species. He needed to know what Archangel intended to do with that power and how they could stop the hunter organisation from getting their hands on it.

Although, the answer to that one might be flying like a dragon out of Hell on a suicide mission to reach her.

He owed Brink a debt he could never repay, but he could at least chip away at it a little by helping him.

Because he had the feeling that Aryanna was something special to Brink.

She was his fated mate.

"Gods, I hope he forgets what the fuck he was doing before he reaches the portal." Lyra tugged him towards the ropes fixed to the left side of the ledge.

Grey stilled.

Gods, Brink was going to forget her again.

The poor bastard.

He couldn't let it happen, but he also couldn't let the male get himself killed by recklessly entering the mortal realm.

"Wait." He pulled Lyra back into the cave, found a pad on one of the dead scientists, and ripped a few sheets out.

He wrote on them in big letters Brink wouldn't be able to miss, and spread them across the floor of the cave, leaving him a message, sure he would return to this place.

Lyra stood over him, her eyes on what he was doing.

When he had finished, he stood and admired his work.

"Brink. Her name is Aryanna. She's your fated one. Archangel might have her. Take this note to King Thorne of the Third Realm. I owe you and I'll help you get her back. Grey." She looked across at him, and smiled. "You big softie."

Grey shrugged. "He'll remember us at least, and hopefully that'll convince him to speak with Thorne. I'll tell Thorne all I know so he'll keep an eye out for a forgetful black dragon. I get the feeling that Brink is the key to awakening her, and that means we need to wait for him to make his move."

He held his hand out to her.

His mission was done. He had an answer for his brother, but more importantly, he had fulfilled his mission to protect Lyra from the fallen angel bent on enslaving her and now all that was left was getting her out of Hell.

Until a black dragon came knocking on Thorne's door, he would return to his world and continue his research into Archangel, sure that Talon would be right there with him, and so would the others at Underworld.

Together, they would arm themselves with all the knowledge they could, they would prepare themselves and they would form an army so powerful Archangel couldn't possibly hope to succeed.

They would be the victor in whatever battle lay ahead of them.

He was sure of it.

Lyra slipped her hand into his. "Let's go home."

As she led him from the cave, those words rang in his heart and had something dawning on him.

That place he had been trying to find since Maya and Talon had left the pride was at Lyra's side, and wherever she went was where he needed to be.

Because she was his home.

CHAPTER 18

Lyra tried to contain her smile as she glanced through the door at Grey where he sprawled across her bed, face down on the furs, a soft grunt escaping him as his nose wriggled and his legs twitched. What was he dreaming in there?

He had faded during their journey to her cabin, the fight and whatever magic Brink had poured into him to heal him taking its toll. She hadn't even had a chance to show him around her home. The moment he had spotted the double bed, he had walked towards it, fallen onto it face-first and dropped straight off to sleep.

That had been two days ago.

Every night when she crawled into bed beside him, he growled, rolled onto his side and pulled her against him, spooning her, his arm banded tightly across her bare stomach.

Every morning she had to wrestle free of his vice-like grip and weather a lot of growls and disgruntled snarls.

When she finally extricated herself, he would flop onto his front and settle again.

She finished washing in the tub in the small bathroom adjacent to her bedroom, stood and let the warm soapy water roll off her, and then stepped out and dried herself off. She slipped into a pair of dark blue-grey shorts and a white tank, and padded quietly out of the bathroom and through the bedroom into the living room at the front of the cabin.

Snow drifted across the windows on either side of the door, the fall heavy enough that the world was going white.

She would have to get supplies in before the weather turned for the worse and she was cut off from the nearest town. She didn't mind the run to it in her hellcat form, but she hated the long trek back pulling a sled of goods through the snow.

She glanced to her right as the light dimmed. The fire was getting low. She snatched a few small logs from the stack as she passed it, rounded the worn dark brown couch and crouched in front of the wood burner. She lifted the door latch, placed the wood in and cleared some of the ash, and then closed the door again.

The living room instantly brightened as the hungry fire devoured the fuel and she breathed a sigh at the comforting warmth that greeted her, and the scent of wood smoke.

Grey growled.

She rose onto her feet and crossed the room back to the bedroom, and peered in, checking on him.

He flipped onto his front and kicked at the furs.

She knew it was a bit warm, but she didn't want him getting cold while he was recovering. Even tigers could get sick.

Lyra went to him and sat on the left side of the bed facing him, propping her bent right leg on the mattress and resting her left foot on the wooden floor. She leaned over him and gently brushed the rogue strands of his silver hair from his forehead, a different sort of warmth curling through her as she studied him.

Her male.

Her mate.

He was even more gorgeous in her bed, his face soft with sleep, all of his worries and cares swept from it and leaving him at peace.

He had watched over her in Hell, had done his best to take care of her and protect her.

Now it was her turn to take care of him.

His eyelids fluttered, and then slowly lifted, revealing the pale blue eyes that had entranced her from the very first time she had looked into them.

He blinked a few times as he looked at her, those eyes sleep-filled but gradually clearing as he woke up. A groggy frown pinched his eyebrows together.

"Shit," he muttered and lifted his left hand and rubbed at his face. "Sorry for falling asleep on you like that."

Lyra shrugged and smiled. "No need to apologise. I slept a little myself… or at least I tried to. It wasn't easy with you pulling me around like a ragdoll."

His cheeks pinkened, and she wondered how long it would be before he stopped feeling embarrassed whenever she talked about things like that. He was new to this, but she never would have guessed from the way he had spooned her like a demon, his long body pressed firmly against hers all night.

He stretched, stopped halfway through as his backside pressed into the furs, and his eyes popped wide. He propped himself up on his elbows and looked down the length of his body, and the pink on his cheeks darkened to red.

"I didn't want you being uncomfortable." She wasn't sure why she felt a need to explain how he had come to be naked, or why her face heated as he stared at her, surprise in his eyes.

"I think you just wanted a good look," he grumbled, but his tone was light and teasing, and she pushed his right shoulder.

It seemed he was already working his way towards losing that sweet and charming innocent edge.

He slumped back into the bed with a sigh, and looked as if he might fall asleep for another two days.

No chance.

He was awake now, and he was staying awake. She'd had two days of getting a 'good look' at him from all angles, and that meant she had spent two days fired up. Horny as hell. Whenever she had tried to cover him, he had kicked the covers away, exposing himself again.

She had started to get the impression that even in sleep, he wanted her eyes on him, and only him.

He wanted to make sure he was the only male she wanted.

As if she could ever want another.

He was the only one for her.

"How are you feeling?" She pressed her hand to his forehead and his eyes slipped shut, a contented sigh escaping him.

"Like a train ran me over. A very long train. And it reversed back over me too." His deep voice had a gravelly edge that did wicked things to her, had her imagining him husking naughty things in her ear in that voice.

She didn't think he was ready for that sort of thing though.

"How long was I out?" He flicked his eyes open, locked them with hers and sent a hot shiver over her skin.

She noted that he made no move to cover himself.

He wanted her to look.

He lifted his arms above his head, settled his hands behind his head and stared at her.

A blatant invitation.

She was starting to get the feeling she wasn't the only one horny as hell.

She ran an appreciative glance down the length of his body, tracing broad pectorals and firm abs, and that enticing ridge of muscle over his hips that lured her gaze downwards.

His cock twitched.

A tremor of need went through her.

"Two days," she muttered, lost in imagining him seizing hold of her, sweeping her under him and giving her a repeat performance of their time in Hell against that boulder.

She wasn't sure she would ever look at rocks the same.

"Shit." Grey shot up in bed. "I need to call my brother."

She glared at him, trying to make it painfully clear that he needed to do something else.

He needed to tend to his mate.

But it was sweet that he wanted to speak with his brother and tell him what he had discovered to alleviate the curiosity that was probably driving him mad.

"There's a phone in the nearest town." Which was miles away, and meant a long journey, and she was damned if she would survive it if she didn't crawl on his lap and scratch the itch she had for him before they left.

"Where's my pack?" He looked for it, blue eyes scanning the room, an edge to his feelings that said he remembered how far away that town was and wouldn't survive delaying making love to her that long either.

She fished it from the floor beside her.

He snatched it, rifled through it and pulled out a phone.

"I doubt you'll get service."

He looked past the phone at her. "You don't know for sure?"

She shrugged and gestured to her small cabin. "I don't own a phone. I don't own much at all."

"We need to change that." The phone screen lit up, brightening his eyes. "Come on. Ha. No bars, but it's not a big fat no."

He did something, and then brought the phone to his ear.

She could hear it ringing.

"Talon?"

A male voice answered. It was more of a shout. He sounded angry. Or perhaps just worried.

"The line is crappy." Grey frowned at his phone and then plastered it back against his ear.

She lowered her gaze from his face to his chest and lost track of his conversation as she studied him, memorised the way his muscles moved as he raked fingers over his hair and as he spoke.

She couldn't stop herself from moving onto her knees on the bed and leaning over him.

His conversation faltered as she pressed a kiss to his right pectoral, biting back a moan at the feel of his firm flesh beneath her lips. His gaze dropped to her, burned into her together with the spike in his feelings, in the need she could sense in him.

She swept her lips across his chest and then downwards, carefully exploring every muscle on his abdomen so she didn't miss a single one.

His eyes tracked her.

"A meeting," he breathed, a little distant as he watched her kissing down his stomach. Talon sounded less than happy on the other end of the phone. Grey cleared his throat. "I am paying attention."

He wasn't.

The rigid length that pressed against her ribs as she moved to straddle his legs said every drop of his focus was on her and not his brother.

"I'll be there," he muttered. "I won't be alone."

She lifted her eyes to his, rested her chin on his stomach and smiled at the way he looked at her. He wasn't letting her out of his sight.

She had been to London a few times.

It would be nice to see it again.

And maybe meet his brother.

She lowered her lips to Grey's stomach again and kept kissing downwards. When her breasts rubbed his hard cock, he swallowed hard and shifted his hips, drove it between them and bit down on his lower lip.

Talon said something.

Grey just swiped his thumb across the screen, dropped the phone on the bed, and fisted his hand in her hair.

"Vixen," he muttered.

The phone rang. Grey ignored it, fire in his eyes as he stared at her and thrust his cock between her breasts.

She smiled and dropped her lips, and kept moving downwards.

She halted before she reached where he wanted her to be.

He groaned. "Stop torturing me."

She grinned, lowered her head and swept her tongue up the length of his rigid shaft. He moaned and shuddered, hips rising to meet her touch and broad shoulders pressing into the bed.

"Gods," he breathed, and she licked him again, swirled her tongue around the blunt head and flicked. He bucked and groaned, his face screwing up and his hand tightening in her hair. "Lyra."

He sounded more serious than delirious.

She lifted her head and found him staring at her, his blue eyes holding a nervous edge.

"I… what… I mean… now you're home…"

She sat up astride his legs. He was nervous, and he hadn't been a second ago. But then, he had been thinking with his little head, and it looked as if he was using his big one now.

"What's the matter?" She stroked his sides, wanting to help him find his voice, because he could talk to her about anything.

It dawned on her what he wanted to say.

"You know how you always took care of your sister, and now that role has ended?" A role she had realised had meant a lot to him and losing it had left him adrift, unsure what to do with himself.

He smiled but it was solemn. "It's strange only having to take care of myself."

"But that isn't the case."

He frowned. "It isn't?"

Lyra shook her head, leaned over him and planted her hands against the pillows on either side of his head.

"If you would like to… you could take care of me too… and I'd take care of you."

His blue eyes went impossibly wide.

And she fell a little bit more in love with him.

"I could?" He stared up at her, and she wanted to box him for being surprised that she would want that.

She had never relied on a male for anything, but she had the feeling she might enjoy relying on Grey.

Being with Grey.

"Someone needs to have my back when we take down Archangel, and I can't think of anyone I want to do that more than you, Grey. I want you at my side when we fight, and I want you at my side when times are quiet. I want you there every hour of the day and every second of the night." She pressed her forehead to his and breathed against his lips. "I want you there forever."

He swallowed hard. "You mean that?"

She nodded. "With all my heart."

He growled and she squeaked as he rolled her onto her back and pinned her to the bed.

"Besides, you swore to protect me," she whispered.

His eyes gained a bright blue corona around his pupils, a hint of fire that she loved seeing in them.

"I did... and I will... I'll protect you forever, Lyra... but I'm greedy." His expression turned wary, solemn again, and he lightly stroked his fingers across her throat. "It's not a collar... but I need to know you're mine and only mine."

Gods.

She needed that too, with a ferocity that stole her breath, had been eating away at her the past two days. She had spent them figuring out how to approach him about it, and instead he had been the one to approach her.

"You're not alone, Grey." She lifted her hands and cupped his cheeks in her palms, and she saw the fire that burned in her eyes reflected in his, all of her feelings echoed in them. "I need it too, and I don't want to wait. I know that's what you're going to say, because you have a big heart in here."

She pressed one hand to his chest and felt that heart beating against it, racing as he took in everything she was saying.

"I'm not leaving this cabin until you're mine, and I'm yours, because if a female so much as looks at you, I'll kill them," she whispered. "So, be mine... forever?"

"When you put it that way." A small smile tugged at his lips. "I suppose I should, in the interest of saving lives."

"You'll be having to save your own life if you keep on like that." She growled playfully at him.

His smile dropped, his expression shifting towards serious again. "I'll be yours... and you'll be mine. We'll both bear the marks, and bear them proudly, and all the world will know that I love you."

"And I love you."

He growled and seized her lips, and she instantly looped her arms around his head and held him to her, tried to pull him closer as a need to stake that claim on him swept through her.

He slipped his hands beneath her tank, pushed it up over her breasts and broke away from her lips. She gasped as he pulled her right nipple into his mouth and sank into the furs, surrendering to him. He teased it with his tongue, flicking it back and forth, sending shiver after shiver over her skin and cranking up the tightness that began low in her belly.

It became heat when he helped her strip her top off, his need flowing through her, laced with a desperate edge that was there in his actions as he tossed her top aside and attacked her shorts, eager to bare her.

She unbuttoned them for him and shimmied them down her hips, and when she tucked her legs up in front of her, between them, to pull them off over her feet, he caught her behind her knees. She slowed, aware of his eyes on her, of the position she was in, and pulled her shorts off and dropped them.

She stared at her legs, waiting for him to make his move, to gather the courage as his heart pounded, need spiking in his veins and flowing into her.

He slowly slid his palms up her calves and caught hold of her ankles, and his eyes burned into her as he parted them, his gaze locked on the apex of her thighs. He groaned as she opened for him, that hunger she could feel in him blazing hotter and burning through her too as he set her on fire with just a look.

There was so much need in his eyes.

He dropped, sank between her thighs and speared her with his tongue.

She bucked up, body singing his praises as her legs fell to rest on his back and her right hand shot down to grip his silver hair.

"Grey." She rocked against his tongue, moaned in time with him as he stroked and teased her, sending her shooting high into the stratosphere.

Gods, she wasn't sure she would ever get enough of him.

He lapped downwards, ran the flat of his tongue hard up the length of her and tore another strained gasp from her lips.

Damn, her tiger was a fast learner.

She slipped her eyes shut and gripped the pillow with her other hand as he brushed his fingers across her core, and slowly eased two inside.

He growled, his shoulders tensing, pleasure rolling through his emotions.

Because she was already wet with need of him.

She had been ready from the moment he had asked her to mate with him, desperate to make it happen so he could finally be hers, and she would finally be his.

He managed three thrusts of his fingers before need got the better of him.

She squeaked as he flipped her onto her front, his feral growl lighting up her blood, a command to submit to him. She growled right back, making it clear that she wasn't going down without a fight.

He tugged her hips up and she barked out a moan as he swept his tongue over her, spread her and speared her with his fingers again.

Her front half sagged into the bed, bliss washing through her to sedate her.

Fine, maybe she would submit to him, because it felt good, so good she wanted to just lay there and take it, let him do as he wanted with her because she felt sure he would make it feel incredible.

He palmed her backside as he stroked her with his tongue, his growls vibrating against her, adding to her pleasure.

When he removed his fingers from her and clutched both of her buttocks, and spread her, she gripped the furs and couldn't stop herself from moaning into them, couldn't keep her hips from rocking as the heat of his gaze scorched her, promising things to come.

He groaned and stroked her so softly, so slowly, that it drove her mad.

His tongue probed her core just as she was about to growl at him, and it came out as a low strangled moan.

"Grey."

His deep growl told her that he could feel her need and swore that he would satisfy it.

He rose to his knees behind her.

Her breath came quicker, anticipation stoking the fire inside her, and she looked over her shoulder at him.

He was glorious as he knelt behind her, long cock jutting towards her and that hungry look in his eyes, one laced with a need to dominate her.

To claim her as his mate.

He stared deep into her eyes, gripped his length and edged his hips towards hers.

She forced herself to hold his gaze as he nudged inside her, as he sank deeper and stretched her, filling all of her, completing her.

Gods.

It heightened her pleasure, had her soaring higher still, on the verge of finding release before he had even done anything.

He stilled inside her, his hands coming down on her hips and then palming her backside, and she moaned in time with him, savouring the feel of him inside her and the connection that bloomed between them.

It wasn't enough though.

She needed more from him.

She reached a hand beneath herself and he grunted as she found his balls. As she pressed her fingers to a spot below them, he growled and shuddered, and his hips shot forwards, driving him deeper into her.

He snatched her hand and leaned over her, pinning her to the bed with his weight as he spread his knees apart and sank lower. She moaned as he planted one hand in the small of her back and pressed down, shifting the angle and sending sparks skittering along her nerves.

"Lyra," he murmured, lost to his passion as he drove into her, sending her out of her mind.

She moaned in response, wasn't sure she could form words as he thrust slow and deep, hit every part of her and had her breath coming faster still, her heart thundering. She gripped the furs and he drove deeper, harder, a soft grunt leaving him with each meeting of their hips, every slap of their flesh against each other.

It wasn't enough.

She growled at him, demanding more.

He flashed fangs and snarled right back at her, plunged deeper and harder, faster. She clutched the furs and moaned each time he filled her, every powerful stroke that spoke of his strength stoking the fire inside her, the inferno that threatened to rage out of control.

More.

She arched back against him, earning a snarl. He pressed harder on her back, grasped her hip in a bruising grip, and moved faster still, his pants filling the bedroom as control slipped from him.

It slipped from her too.

She sank deep into her instincts as they rose inside her, demanding her mate satisfy her, served her and claimed her.

As if he had felt her need, his hand came down on the nape of her neck.

She shivered, anticipation rolling through her, need that had her growling at him, snapping and pushing him.

He growled and pulled her up to him, caging her with one arm across her breasts as he drove into her. He seized her hair with his other hand, tugging it up to expose her nape.

Gods.

She needed it.

Might die if he didn't do it now.

She snarled at him, one last push she couldn't contain.

A fierce demand.

He roared.

Sank his fangs into her nape.

Drove deep.

Pain exploded within her, but as it swept through her it became pleasure that stole her breath, had her shaking violently in his arms as she climaxed, stars winking across her vision and her heart stopping as she opened her mouth.

As she roared.

He growled against her nape, one long continuous rumble as he held her in his fangs and plunged his cock into her.

She quivered and moaned, trembled as he throbbed inside her, as his warmth filled her and the connection between them grew stronger, tying them together.

A link they could never break.

She wanted it stronger still.

She wore his mark.

He would wear hers.

The world would know he loved her.

And she loved him.

She twisted in his arms.

His growl of displeasure lasted all of a second.

The time it took for her to land behind him, reach around him to seize his cock, and sink her fangs into his nape.

He roared, arching in her fangs, his bliss rolling through her as he spilled in her hand, his length pulsing hard in time with the tremors that swept through her, a release born of the taste of his blood on her tongue and the pleasure she had given him.

When the final tremors had rocked her, and he was still in her hand, she managed to convince herself to pry her jaws open and release him.

Even though she didn't want to.

She pulled her fangs from his neck, and lapped at the wounds, clearing the blood away and sealing them.

A contented purr rumbled up her throat.

She could feel him, all of him. She could feel his satisfaction, and the pleasure she had given him, and all the love he held for her.

He made a low coughing sound in his throat, one that called to her.

She rounded him, lifted her hair for him and gave him what he wanted.

He ran his tongue over her nape and the shivers that chased through her threatened to get her going again but there would be time for that later. Right now, she wanted to savour this moment with him, this start of a new beginning together.

When he was done, he gathered her in his arms, and twisted with her, bringing her down onto the bed facing him.

She stared into those beautiful blue eyes that told her everything.

Never had been able to hide his feelings from her.

He loved her, and that love was eternal.

He would protect her, to the end of time.

And he would never stop looking at her as if she was everything to him, as if she was his entire world and he couldn't live without her.

She had been through hell, and so had he, but now they were together.

And she silently swore that she would love him eternally, would protect him no matter what, and she would never stop looking at him as if he was her everything.

She would make him feel the way he made her feel.

Treasured by her tiger.

The End

ABOUT THE AUTHOR

Felicity Heaton is a New York Times and USA Today best-selling author who writes passionate paranormal romance books. In her books she creates detailed worlds, twisting plots, mind-blowing action, intense emotion and heart-stopping romances with leading men that vary from dark deadly vampires to sexy shape-shifters and wicked werewolves, to sinful angels and hot demons!

If you're a fan of paranormal romance authors Lara Adrian, J R Ward, Sherrilyn Kenyon, Gena Showalter, Larissa Ione and Christine Feehan then you will enjoy her books too.

If you love your angels a little dark and wicked, the best-selling Her Angel series is for you. If you like strong, powerful, and dark vampires then try the Vampires Realm series or any of her stand-alone vampire romance books. If you're looking for vampire romances that are sinful, passionate and erotic then try the best-selling Vampire Erotic Theatre series. Or if you prefer huge detailed worlds filled with hot-blooded alpha males in every species, from elves to demons to dragons to shifters and angels, then take a look at the new Eternal Mates series.

If you have enjoyed this story, please take a moment to contact the author at **author@felicityheaton.co.uk** or to post a review of the book online

Connect with Felicity:
Website – http://www.felicityheaton.co.uk
Blog – http://www.felicityheaton.co.uk/blog/
Twitter – http://twitter.com/felicityheaton
Facebook – http://www.facebook.com/felicityheaton
Goodreads – http://www.goodreads.com/felicityheaton
Mailing List – http://www.felicityheaton.co.uk/newsletter.php

FIND OUT MORE ABOUT HER BOOKS AT:
http://www.felicityheaton.co.uk

Printed in Great Britain
by Amazon